OVER THE SEA'S EDGE

by the same author

Down from the Lonely Mountain
California Indian Tales

Beneath the Hill

The Sleepers

The Change-Child

The Daybreakers

Mindy's Mysterious Miniature

OVER THE SEA'S EDGE

Jane Louise Curry

Illustrated by Charles Robinson

Harcourt Brace Jovanovich, Inc.
New York

ISBN 0-15-259010-2
Library of Congress Catalog Card Number: 70-152693
Printed in the United States of America
B C D E F G H I J

The seventeen lines of poetry on page 62 are a translation by Gwyn Williams of the medieval Welsh poem, "Pais Dinogad," and are reprinted with the permission of Curtis Brown Ltd., London, from *An Introduction to Welsh Poetry*, published by Faber and Faber.

My heart wishes with longing for flowers,
For laughter and the song of one,
Or two.
I, Micalo,
I suffer with this weight of golden flowers,
The crystal rabbit, the jade bird,
The stone heart.
I cannot warm them in my hands.
I cannot warm
My hands.
My heart longs for one fragile flower
On the green hills of Tajín,
And no Law but
Flowering.

—"SONG OF THE EXILE" from the
Twelfth Royal Book of Tajín

Contents

I
GWYNET

1

The Boy

Three days running, Dave Reese had seen the boy, and now he was an uneasy presence threading through his dream. Dave mumbled a wordless protest and buried his head under the pillow, but could not shake free of the dream. Its images simply shifted, like chips of bright color in a kaleidoscope, and began again at the beginning.

He hadn't seen the boy close up the first two times: only from a considerable distance, in the shadow between two trees. It was as if the boy had followed Dave into Hatch's Wood, keeping parallel to the path but safely distant. Each time Dave had turned away nervously and hurried on toward Westover Road and school, only to stop after a moment and look behind him—into an empty wood. Yesterday he had back-tracked to scout around. Nothing. It was bewildering, engrossing.

The image that took shape in his mind's eye, growing out of that distant, blurred figure, was at once vivid and indistinct: long hair—much longer than Dave had managed to get his own before Mrs. Bellick, the housekeeper, made his father order him off to the barber shop—a baggy tunic, faded blue with X's all over it, a little like the African dashiki shirts some of the older black boys at the public high school wore; and boots—boots wound around with leather string, shabby and exotic. Dave's initial alarm had been drowned in envy. Anyone who didn't have slave drivers like old Trumbull and some of the other teachers at

Fettles Academy, and who wasn't made to comb his hair and change into a freshly ironed shirt every time he turned around, was bound to have time on his hands. Time to try for catfish from the riverbank, maybe take a Saturday pleasure-boat ride downstream to Cincinnati. Even build a raft with driftwood and derelict oil drums. Yes, build a raft and camp out on one of the islands in the Ohio. Dave had always dreamed of doing that. The islands fascinated him.

He guessed the boy would have a guitar, too. It took time to learn to play the guitar. Time, and something better than a fifteen-dollar instrument glued together like a matchbox that cracked all the way down the back as soon as cold weather came and the central heating was turned on.

Dave had longed for boots, too, but the best he could manage in the face of his father's resistance to "fads" was to save up and send away for a cheap pair of Indian desert boots from a trading post in New Mexico that advertised in *Fantastic Comics* (which he was (a) supposed to have outgrown and (b) not allowed to have in any case). The boots had been a violent, horrible shade of Easter turquoise, but soft and comfortable, almost as luxurious as going barefoot. A week after they came Mrs. Bellick found them and sent them off to the Salvation Army, saying that they were bad for the arches: no support.

Finally, this morning after breakfast when Dave had slammed out the front gate and then turned back to latch it so that he wouldn't come in for another reminder about carelessness—this very morning Dave had seen the dim, familiar figure much closer, watching from the Abernethys' tree-shaded driveway. Shyness and all, Dave would have waved and called to him if some warning instinct had not weighted his hand and closed his throat. For three seconds that seemed three ages, he stood rooted while his brain sluggishly registered what it was that he saw, and then he turned blindly on his heel and hurried down the street. At the corner he turned into De Soto Road and broke into a run. It was the long way around, but he meant to keep clear of Hatch's Wood. You might as well be on the moon in there. Half a block before the Junior High School he slowed again, passing it with an air of nonchalance that masked a fierce jealousy of the noise and color and straggling groups of boys and girls exchanging good-humored insults at the gate. He knew one or two from back in the sixth grade, but only Meroly Gladwyn, whose hair was stringier than ever, recognized him.

"Look, everybody! It's a four-eyed, chicken-hearted bookworm," she sang.

"Ah, how tender! Going to get its ears and fingernails inspected at the Bookworms' *Nur*sery School!" shrilled a second voice. The others laughed and then mercifully lost interest.

Once he was out of sight around the corner on Westover Road, Dave found he could not stop the shaking in his knees. He had to sit down on the curb behind a parked car and put his head between his legs. He would have to run to get to Fettles Academy before the late bell, but for the moment he could not go another step. Part of the trembling was fright, part was fury at having been startled into fright. The rest was humiliation at the familiar taunts of the kids his age who went to public school instead of the Academy.

At least the boy would not follow him here. There was too much traffic, too much bustle. Dave took off his glasses, dropped them in the gutter, groped frantically, and then shakily began to polish them on his necktie. Four blocks to go. For the first time, Fettles' red brick Gothic buildings and the headmaster hovering at the door in the hope of catching latecomers would seem warm and welcoming. Well, *safe*, at least.

The boy. Dave had been right enough about the boy's long hair and his clothes, but what had been exciting at a distance was something else again when seen a bit closer. It wasn't the far-out clothes. They were still enviably cool even if they did look moth-eaten and slept-in. Except it was only a tunic and dirty bare legs, not a shirt over tight trousers. Afterward it reminded Dave of the picture illustrating *tunica* in the copy of the *First Latin Dictionary for Schools* that Mr. Trumbull kept on his desk for the boys to use in Latin class. But as Dave stared at the figure in the Abernethys' driveway, he had been aware more of the dull silver gleam of a pendant, strung on a cord around the boy's neck, and the eyes that watched him so hungrily. Eager and hungry. The eyes were disquieting enough, sharp and clear and fierce—hawk's eyes that made Dave feel sickeningly rabbitish—but, worse, the pendant had been the double of the one that hung on a string against Dave's own breastbone, hidden under his T-shirt. He had seen the bird shape clearly when it flashed. And he had run.

His own pendant hung heavily against his chest through the rest of the day, a warm, sweaty weight upon his mind that ruined a history quiz and a math demonstration and turned Latin translation into a fumbling nightmare. It made one of his usual bad days look like glowing success. Even George Simmons laughed at one mistake, so Dave changed his mind about telling George anything. That left his father to talk to, if he could be caught in an expansive after-a-good-dinner-and-brandy mood.

That evening Mr. Reese tapped the piercework disc thoughtfully and traced with a slow finger the figure that hovered within the silver circle. It had a soaring grace to it, but was stylized almost beyond recognition. Dave thought it looked like a winged man. His father was sure it was a bird. "Mm. Interesting. Unusual work. Scarcely looks Indian; almost European. And you found it last weekend? Ah, in one of the caves overlooking the river up near Poole. Hmph. I used to fool around in those caves myself, before Dad sold off that part of the farm. Found a lot of those arrowheads there. . . . Nothing like this." His voice trailed off as he nodded vaguely toward the framed display of arrowheads on his study wall. "Actually, I suppose you were trespassing if you went over the east field and down to the river. I don't know the people who own the bluffs now. You'll have to ask your Uncle Jim who they are, you know. By rights this doodad is theirs, unless they say you can keep it. A very interesting piece. Very interesting. Um. Might not be a bad idea if I took it up to college tomorrow. Shall we ask the Archaeology Department whether it might be valuable?"

"All right." Dave felt helpless under the force of so much practical, logical commonsense. "But what about that boy?" he ventured. "He *has* been following me . . . ever since Monday."

His father had shifted uncomfortably. "Now, are you sure about that, Dave? I mean, it wasn't just another daydream? You see, I came out through the garage before you turned down De Soto this morning, and I swear there wasn't a soul in sight upstreet, downstreet, or in the Abernethys' driveway." He gave a kindly meant but thoughtlessly cruel suggestion of nursery-rhyme chant to the words.

"No, sir." Dave looked out the window. "Maybe I'm not sure. But can—can I keep the pendant-thing for a while, please?"

"Mm. For now, yes, of course. But I think I will take it in to show it to Tom Mazzioti tomorrow or Monday, if you don't mind." He raised his eyebrows and smiled in one of his heavy-handed attempts at humor. "And if you don't think your *Döppelganger* will mind? Right. Better get at your homework now, friend. I think I'll get in a little polishing on that battery-car article I'm doing for *Scientific Advance*." He handed the medallion over with a puzzled shake of the head. "It beats me. It really does. If you put half as much energy into your schoolwork as you put into your imagination, life would be considerably easier. Sometimes I can't think why I spend good money to send you to a stiffer school. When I was a kid, I would have given my eyeteeth to have the kind of head start you can get at the Academy, but . . ."

But I'm not you. I'm not. Afterward all the words Dave could not say aloud and all the daydreams his father had forgotten, if ever he had them, tumbled together despairingly. *I don't WANT to Structure My Personality Around a Positive Goal.* I *want to . . . to sail down to the Gulf of Mexico on a raft and explore a wilderness and ride with a banner in the winds and . . . and know how to live off trapping and acorns and nuts and berries or whatever, and. . . .* But then, he knew, after you got past twelve, you were supposed to Start Being Practical. Practical people like Mr. Reese never seemed to be content with being practical themselves. Dave supposed they felt it impractical to have other people messing around being impractical. As he played idly with the words, something his father had said returned to strike him like a cold wind.

Döppelganger. What had made him say *Döppelganger?* It meant some sort of double who shadowed you, Dave thought, struggling up out of his daydreams. He could not find the word in his own dictionary and was shy of going to look it up in his father's big *Oxford Third International Dictionary*. He would never hear the end of it. Besides, he told himself, it wasn't so . . . couldn't be. For one thing, the other boy had eyes to see for miles with, and Dave was lost without his glasses. For another . . .

* * *

Döppelganger. The leaves whispered. Dave bit on the rough wool blanket and moaned, and in his dream he stood rooted in the wood and turned slowly, unwillingly, fearful of what he might see.

He saw *himself* standing close behind him.

The other Dave reached out an eager hand to touch his sleeve, but then drew back as if for him, too, fascination and fear were bewilderingly mixed up together. They stood; regarded each other with wonder and envy. The other boy's hair—like Dave's, dark and curly—hung in tangles to his shoulders. The same short, stocky figure, the same level dark brows, the same snub nose. Only the eyes and a crooked white scar along one cheekbone were different. The boy's belt was a length of rope frayed into tassels at the ends, and the legs above the ragged boots were criss-crossed with angry welts. At the top of one boot the worn bone handle of a knife showed, and Dave's heart raced with excitement. Then, in the dream, that other Dave tugged the cord around his neck until it broke and clutched the ornament on the cord tightly for a moment before offering it to Dave, as if fearful he would not accept it. But he did, and fumbling to pull out his own in exchange, as an awkward recognition of this strange, compelling other self, Dave awoke with a start to the pounding of his own heart and the hammering of blood in his ears.

For a single wild, breathless, falling moment he could not think where he was, or who. Only when the idea of that sensation, the word "falling" itself, took shape in his mind—only then did he find himself; and the warm darkness closed safely around him. Dave let out a soft sigh of relief and drew his knees up against his chest. The movement was answered by a low whimper, a cold nose, and a warm, snuggling shape.

"Brownie? How'd you get in here? Didn't Dad shut you

in the garage?" He spoke in a whisper and reached out a hand to give the terrier's ears a rub. "Mrs. Bellick'll have a double-barreled fit if she finds you've been up on the bed. Here, come on under . . ." He stopped, startled, his hand on the dog's head.

"Brownie?"

The hair on the broad forehead under his hand bristled. The ears stiffened. The whispered name hung in the darkness.

A faint rasp rose at the back of the dog's throat, a trembling, undecided sound that might become either growl or whine. Dave felt and heard the dog—Brownie?—move nervously backward. *Backward.* Not down from the bed, but backward until there was a sound that might have been—surely not?—the scraping of a large dog's toenails against stone.

Raising up in surprise, Dave struck his elbow a sharp crack on what should have been, *had* to be, his beloved too-soft mattress. ("No support," was Mrs. Bellick's grumble every time she changed the bedclothes.) The first panicky thought as he lay back in alarm—that there could be, *was*, indeed, a strange dog on his bed—died away with the comforting realization that he was not in his own bed but still moving in the shifting dream.

Yet nothing happened. And dreams do not stand still. They shift and slip, evasive as mercury under a curious finger; and so as minutes dragged on, the darkness was more and more a blindfold, less and less a comfort. Dave schooled his breath to a shallow, silent movement and felt his heartbeat slow and soften. His senses sharpened with straining to hear and see. Somewhere—in a corner?—the dog was breathing softly and rapidly almost below the edge of hearing. Dave shrank from the hovering, incredible doubt that thrust at him. He could not be awake! The elbow throbbed, and though his fingers ached to rub it, he kept still and did not move. By the expedient of not moving, he was able not to be certain. By not shifting weight onto hip and shoulder, he kept his scurrying mind from any certainty whether he was in his own bed or incredibly, impossibly, bedded down on a stone floor. The scratchy wool of an unfamiliar blanket, the missing sheet, and a growing awareness of damp and the stink of dog and mildew could almost be reasoned away with tumbled bedclothes, a window left open to the rain, and one of Brownie's unhappy accidents . . . but not the sounds that a sharpened hearing caught. Not the thump of a long tail, soft breathing everywhere, and a sigh from somewhere behind his back that was scarcely doglike. A wisp of hair slipped across his cheek to rest along his nose, and in a sudden terror that he might sneeze, Dave raised a hand to press his upper lip hard against his teeth.

As the spasm passed, his hand jerked. Hair. His own hair? *His own and not his own.* His fingers found the scar and followed it in slow unbelief along the cheekbone to twine themselves in a tangle of curls. There was scarcely any need to slip his free hand under the harsh woolen coverlet to touch the tender weals on his legs or the strings that wound around the boots. His ears drummed with strange night noises until his mind closed against both sound and touch, and he lay staring in the dark . . . until dawn crept under a low door and through its cracks and a distant churchbell tolled six notes to stir a silent world.

There was a faint snigger as a small but bony knee drove into his back. "Ssss. Too late, Dewi! Poor Clerk Dewi! Your old Father Gwillim's praying at his devotions by now. You'll not be getting your precious Latin grammar this morning! And none of his fine milk sops for your breakfast. Hah!" All of this was hissed in a tone of rich satisfaction and followed by a sharp kick. "Here, now, wake you! Half a loaf says I'm in at t' kitchen first."

The low door crashed open, and a small figure bolted out. Dave sat up in a gray half-light in what seemed a low, huddled storeroom or kennel full of yawning, stretching dogs. Moving as if in a dream, not believing it was not a dream, he crawled to the door and looked out on a dim gray world of stone wall, rocky hillside, and dark trees. Across the wide cobbled courtyard a great stone tower pushed against the gray sky, defying both dark and dawn with its banner, a red dragon flapping in the wind.

2
The Trap

Dave stood staring, half afraid to breathe for fear the dream might blow away despite its apparent solidity. Stepping forward, he felt the rough unevenness of cobbles underfoot and looked down with an interest that itself was detached and dreamlike. He saw that his boots gaped at the toes and had been tied around with the leather string because they were a man's boots, and too large. Frightened, he shied away from this strange self and stared about him wildly, trying to fasten on some key to the strangeness of the scene. Everywhere stone and mortar, hill and trees and sky sprang at him, crowding his head with colors and shapes as vivid and new and almost as senseless as a scene in a mirror kaleidoscope. It was as if he had never seen a stone, a hill, a tree before. The crowding sense of each rock's graininess, of the patterns of cobbles and walls, of the first yellowed leaves drifting down through still air to brighten the dull hillside—the rush of detail was bewildering, overwhelming. A hawk wheeling high overhead was as sharp and clear as the red dragon that flew over the castle keep.

"*Y curyll coch,*" Dave whispered, shielding his eyes with cupped hands as he watched its slow, lazy circle. A kestrel. But how did he know that? In a sudden panic he wondered where the name had come from and why it should fall so strangely from his tongue. Why *curyll coch* for "kestrel"?

"Ss-st! Dewi!"

The call, for one motionless, uncomprehending moment, brought Dave skirting close to nightmare. A head appeared at the upper side of the sloping courtyard, strangely disembodied, thrusting up through the cobbles at the base of the great tower. It nodded horribly and made dreadful faces, mouthing soundless words. Dave's bemused and gaping silence seemed to anger it, and with a final horrid shake it disappeared.

In a moment it had popped up again, but less alarmingly, for it turned out to be firmly attached to shoulders and a pair of scrawny arms that beckoned and then pointed insistently to something behind Dave. Belatedly, Dave realized that this was the same small boy who had earlier kneed him in the back. He appeared to be crouching on a stairway that led to an underground level of the tower, and the wild signaling seemed some sort of warning. Dave turned to see what this oddest of dreams might spring upon him next.

The reality was not promising: no offer of adventure, no plea from a distressed damsel. A harsh voice and the clatter of a horse's hoofs on stone rang somewhere on the far side of the building where he now stood—one of several wooden structures huddled by the lower of the castle's towers. The pack of hounds stretched and yawned in the kennel yard, and the last stragglers shouldered through the low door to sniff at the morning and eye Dave speculatively. One circled wide around him to trot with an elaborately casual air toward the small boy hiding on the stair, ignoring the child's frantic attempts to wave him away. Dave felt no urgency, but something moved him to snap his fingers sharply and call in a low tone, "Here, Mailcun! Come, boy."

The dog wheeled obediently and came to his hand, tail thumping, but with a shy nervousness that kept his paws moving in a shifting dance on the pavement. Dave frowned. The dog accused him, dumbly, of omission, of strangeness. But there was no time to puzzle at small riddles. "Hai, sit back! Back," came the bellow from around the corner, and the whinny and stamp of horses was cut off by the clang of an iron-bound stable door.

"In kennel! The lot of you!" Without thinking, Dave raised his right hand in command and whistled a sharp, dropping note. It seemed the most natural of things that the hounds should grin amiably and crowd back into the kennel without coaxing. Dave frowned as he looped the door's rope latch around a metal staple and fastened it with the wooden pin that hung by a string from the staple. He turned slowly. The small boy grinned at him and made an elaborate show of wiping his brow in relief, then stooped to hoist a heavy oak bucket up the last two steps of the deep stairwell.

"Blessed Samson!" roared the voice that a moment before had been cursing a skittish horse. A string of loud oaths rattled across the courtyard, and a burly man, dark and bearded, rounded the corner from the stables in company with a thin youth weighted down by an iron cap and armed with a wicked-looking pike. "Holy Teilo," bellowed the older man, "the hounds not fed yet, and look at our Saint Dewi, gawping there like a fish out of water! That's right. Above us all is Dewi. Him with his Latin scraps and gentle tongue."

The voice curled around Dave like a whiplash. "Well, I'll give you learning, *Dewi sant!* Wasn't it Selyf the Wise said, '*Dyrchfael a wna yspryt yn erbyn kwymp dyn*'? Eh? So you'll be climbing down out of your cloudy visions and giving the brat there a hand with the dogs' meal or I'll write 'Razo' across your backside a sight clearer than it's writ on your shanks. Off with you!"

Dewi sant . . . Saint David. And Selyf was . . . Solomon? *Dyrchfael a wna* . . . Solomon saying that pride grows before a man's fall. . . . Dave's head whirled. Razo's words, like his own and the small boy's before, fell strangely on his ears: a rolling, rich tongue altogether foreign and at the same time—how?—familiar.

"*Move*, church mouse!"

Dave scurried across the sloping yard and bent to grasp one of the heavy bucket's rope handles. It was full to the brim with meat and bones, bread and table scraps. Together, the two boys lifted and ran, straining, shoulders stiff and arms rigid, knees pumping. As the bucket—it was nearer the size of a tub—thumped down beside the kennel door, Dave heard himself murmur, "Thanks, Elisy. I wasn't awake."

The smaller boy looked up at him shyly. "I *did* eat your breakfast. But I was sorry after. Cook said Razo drank too much mead last night again and was feeling it something fierce, so I was feared he would be beating you if the hounds was all over the place before they was fed." He hesitated, then ventured in a lower whisper, "*Was* you having a vision, Dewi? A holy one like Saint Teilo? Or . . ." His eyes shone. "Or about the place where wagons go without horses to pull 'em, and the hawks are silver, and where the town is, the one that's all castles and great houses?"

Dave went cold all over. "Hush! That was no more than a dream, Elisy."

The words were no sooner out than his tongue clove to the roof of his mouth. *Elisy. He had said it again. That was the boy's name, but how should David Reese know that? And how should he be understanding and answering in this tongue that was so unlike English?* Trembling, Dave dumped the thick mess from the bucket into a stone gutter by the kennel. Elisy pulled the wooden pin from the door catch. The hounds tumbled out, and in a moment they were tearing at the meat, the bones, and each other.

But then again, why shouldn't he know the name Elisy? Why shouldn't his hands and feet and tongue know what they were doing? It was all a part of the dream. The dream decided what he would say, and how. He had only to go along with it, be both actor and spectator. He hooked his thumbs in the rope knotted at his waist and kept his eyes on the snarling, struggling dogs, uncomfortably aware of the boy Elisy's watchful curiosity.

"Curse you, priestling! Have y' no eyes in your skull? The bitch has torn Mailcun's ear and you stand by with your head in the clouds. Oi!"

Razo, the master of horses and hounds, had come up quietly behind the boys, loosening his braided leather belt as he came. Wielding it with obvious enjoyment, he bellowed his way into the melee to put a stop to the fighting. Dave caught one lash of the belt on his thighs as Razo's rough curse was flung at his head, and more after the hounds were separated. Elisy, with great presence of mind, disappeared into the empty kennel.

The thin soldier laughed as Dave, speechless with disbelief and anger and thoroughly awake at last, backed away from the horse master's flailing belt. The noise brought other watchers. Laughter and curses were mixed with the barking of dogs and with shouts of encouragement and derision from the cook and his helpers, crowding the stairwell and the small ground-level windows of the basement kitchens. Half-dressed soldiers lounged in their barracks door to watch, and in a few moments the uproar had drawn sleepy faces to the tower windows. Someone above emptied a dish of apple cores on the cook's head and shrieked—to no avail—for quiet.

It was not a dream. The pain in Dave's legs was too sharp, too sudden, too deep not to break a dream and wake him, trembling, in his own bed. How could it be anything but real? Dave could have screamed at the sluggishness of his wits. *Don't let it go its own way. Do something!* He had fallen into a game for which he did not know the rules and was caught in the center of a cruel entertainment where a well-laid-on blow or a stumbling escape were cheered alike, in a world that was a confusion of viciousness and absurdity. In the moment of retreat between one stinging blow and the next, he thought wildly, *He's left me here and taken my place because of this. This, and some daydream of being a scholar. And Dad and old Trumbull won't see his oddness, they'll be so glad of him.* Adventure—so long wished for—had a bitter, salt taste. He had bit his lip until it bled.

Perhaps it was shock; perhaps it was because he, unlike that other Dewi, had never been harried or humiliated; certainly it was without thinking that Dave picked himself up from the rough cobbles to stand unsteadily erect, arms folded, an angry light in his eyes and his nostrils white and pinched. His knees were a little shaky, but he held his ground. Even a cruel game takes two to play and only one to change the rules. It was Razo's turn to look absurd. The motley audience grew quiet, and Razo faltered, balked by this new turn. His hand dropped.

"Check!" The voice that cut across the courtyard was light and amused. "The worm turneth! I do love to see a worm turn!"

The speaker, a young man, stood at the top of the stair

that climbed to the doorway of the Great Hall in the castle keep. He wore a tunic patterned with large checks of brilliant blue and green, and a long sword hung from his silver-studded belt. Like the others, he was barefoot. His reddish-yellow hair was trimmed evenly to a length a little below his ears, and gold rings winked on his fingers. *A prince,* Dave thought. *A prince like a lazy, blue-eyed marmalade cat, a cat with sharp claws.*

"Well, horse master," said the young man. "What is your move? Surely your courage will stretch a little further? You have roused the sons of Ywein and their ladies from their beds. Prince Iorwerth's cook must get to his kitchen, and this ragtag of a guard should be snuffling at their feeding trough—where their sergeant has orders for them, and a double ration of ale. But you, horse master, are quite free to go on with your game." He bowed.

"Aah! You know what you can do with your fine airs and fripperies, Prydyt y Moch!" Razo spat and turned on his heel.

Dave stood shivering in the center of the silent, emptying yard. The sun over the eastern hills touched the tower and the bright dragon banner with gold, and sheep grazed on the peaceful slopes.

"Prydyt y Moch?" asked Dave. He shuddered as the splendid young man smeared the welts on his arms and legs with butter begged from the cook.

"Aye, that's me. Prydyt y Moch. The Poet of the Pigs." The blue eyes crinkled warmly. "Llywarch ap Llewelyn if you are inclined to be formal. Llywarch the pig-boy who saw in a vision he was meant to be a warrior and a poet. And you? I would guess you are the dog-boy the old priest hopes to send one day to Bangor to be made a scholar. Dewi, isn't it? Sorry!" he said as Dave flinched. "The lout broke the skin there. The boots have saved you from worse. But do you always go shod in fine weather?"

"They belonged to my father," Dave answered shortly. He had allowed himself to be led across the courtyard to the low south wall overlooking the valley below. The poet —if that was truly what he was—had said that he wanted to keep an eye on the river road. While Llywarch did his doctoring, Dave watched; and then in silence they shared the lookout and a large bowl of bread and milk.

"*Should* I know you?" Dave asked at last, warily.

The ginger-colored eyebrows shot up. "Not at all." Llywarch sighed, mocking at himself. "Not even if you were a student of poetry as well as of Latin dialogues. No, we poets and warriors who serve Prince Hywel are like the sapling oaks caught in the shade of the beech tree. Our warrior-poet-prince can outfight and outrhyme any man in Gwynet." He grinned. "And he gives us little leisure. Now, your life here at Dolwydlan—or rather, not yours, but your Prince Iorwerth's—pleases me. A little rough, perhaps, but easy-going. And Iorwerth has no house poet. Perhaps I shall ask him to take me on." The young man scanned the river road with his bright cat eyes.

"Why tell me all this?" Dave wiped his mouth on the back of his wrist. "And who are we watching for?" Each precious bit of information was a piece of ground grown firm beneath Dave's uncertain feet. Prince Iorwerth was lord of this castle. But who was Prince Hywel? "Why tell me?" he repeated. "I might go tattling to your Prince Hywel."

"Might you? Then tell and be welcome. I am a free man." Llywarch turned to lean back against the wall, resting on his elbows. "Flatter all princes and be owned by none, I say. It's a good enough life, for old Ywein Gwynet has sired enough princes to support every poet worth salt in all the north of Wales. Life is never dull adventuring with Hywel, but a favor or a poem now and again for

Prince Davyt, say, or Rodri: that is pleasant work, too." He turned his hand so that the stones in the gold rings flashed blood and wine-colored in the reaching sunlight.

Dave frowned. "Prince Iorwerth and Prince Hywel are brothers. Their father Ywein is the king of Gwynet, then? Gwynet in the north of Wales. And Hywel must be visiting here." He nodded in emphasis to each thought, as if he were committing history dates to memory, and did not realize that he had spoken aloud. Llywarch watched him with open curiosity.

"It is true, then, what the old priest Gwillim fears," said Llywarch with every appearance of delight. "Scholarship has addled the boy's wits! Where are you from, young Dewi? And how does a lad with literary ambitions come to be a dog-boy? Or should I ask how a dog-boy catches a thirst for learning?"

Dave decided that a vague version of the truth—his own truth—would be no more dangerous than invention. There could be advantages in a reputation for oddity. "I'm not really so thirsty for it," he announced. "It was my father's idea. He once wanted to be a scholar. But that was before the war."

Llywarch was interested. "Did he fight against the English, then? Was he with us on that best of days, at the pass of Cefn yr Ogof, when we ambushed King Henry and drove the English from Tegeigl?"

"N-no. He—he was in France." When had Wales been at war with England? Dave wished the history he remembered was not such a jumble of disconnected snippets. *France?*

"France?" The poet looked at him sharply and then reached out a hand faster than a striking snake to pull the cord and the silver medallion from under Dave's tunic. Almost as quickly he thrust it back out of sight. "A sea bird? A pretty trinket. And a strange boy. But what is all this kitchen gossip about visions? The household thinks you mad, you know. Your Prince Iorwerth asked the priest about it after dinner last night in hall. I would have a care if I were you. Poets and priests must be as politic with their dreams as with their flattery. Too strange a vision, or even a holy one ill-timed, can lead to hanging or to burning." Having delivered himself of this solemn warning, the poet hoisted himself onto the low parapet and sat kicking his legs like a boy and grinning. "Come, then! What did you dream that stammagasted them so?"

What had that other Dave—*Dewi,* he amended, pronouncing it to himself as Llywarch and Elisy spoke it—what had Dewi dreamed? *Me. He dreamed me. And home. And I dreamed him. And it all got crossed up somehow.* What on earth had Marietta, Ohio, looked like to that other Dewi?

"Dewi? Tell about the great silver hawks," Elisy prompted. He had crept close to listen. "I like that part best."

Dave—*Dewi*—was cautious. No silver birds or horseless wagons. "Shut you up, Elisy," he said impatiently as he groped for a description that would be safe and satisfying. "It was a real place; a country with a lot of towns, and tall towers, and a wide river that ran all the way down to the sea."

Llywarch's eyes narrowed, and he frowned faintly, as if the words stirred some echo. But that was impossible, Dewi knew.

"Where was this dream country, then?"

"Across the ocean," Dewi answered, taking a deep breath and trusting that such an idea would be thought harmless, however mad, in these Dark Ages—for what other time could this be? Barefoot poets and soldiers, and ladies who threw garbage out of windows? The dragon flag flew bravely, but over a place more like a barnyard than a palace, one that was surely an age away from knights in armor riding on Crusades with ladies' favors fluttering from their helms. "Across the ocean," he repeated. "It's very far away and much bigger than—than France and Spain together. I liked the river best, I think."

Llywarch seemed disappointed. "No marvels? They were all embroidery, then? Ah, well! I suppose two-headed dragons and rivers of gold and milk-white maidens with fishes' tails are gone out of fashion in dreams, are they?" He laughed and gestured toward the river road. "But the world is always full of dreamers of your land to the west. Here comes another of them." Cupping his hands to his mouth, he called out to the tower, "*Llyma varchogyon yn dyuot ar vrys!* Madauc! And coming fast, my lords!"

To Dewi's eyes the five riders appeared as sharp and clear at the far road's head as miniature horsemen held in the palm of the hand. That was perhaps the most unnerving thing about this new self: to be able to see so clearly. To have no glasses meet the finger he so automatically pushed along the bridge of his nose continually startled him. He could make out the details of harness and weapon, even distinguish the features of faces and banners. The foremost banner bore as its device a sea bird, white on a blue field.

"Who is Madauc? Is he one of your princes, too?"

Elisy tapped his head meaningly. Despite the shadow in his eyes that seemed an odd compound of disappointment and pity, Llywarch only drawled, "Why, he's half a monk already, to know so little of the world! Though there are times when I wish I knew less of it. Madauc? Who knows if he be prince or not? Rumor says yes, but she's a wishful dame. Friend Madauc was a member of King Ywein's *teulu,* his bodyguard, and the law is that no member of the *teulu* may be a kinsman of the king. More, Ywein never unbent to give him greeting, even. But Madauc brought such glory on himself when he won against King Henry and the English at Rudlan two years past, and since then in the south, that the old king named him *penteulu*, captain of the guard. That set the tongues wagging over the length and breadth of Gwynet, for, you see, not only may the *penteulu* be a kinsman; but he also stands in for the king in hall and answers to no one else! Lately Ywein has leaned heavily on young Madauc, and how the princes grind their teeth at it, for all the court remarks the new *penteulu's* resemblance to Prince Rien, the best-beloved and most gallant of all the king's sons, who died some twenty-odd years ago. They say half of Ywein's heart died with Rien. This month past Madauc achieved for Ywein Gwynet a great victory against Ywein Kyveilawc, his old enemy. So now, in his pleasure and his illness, the king has recalled Madauc to Aberffraw in Von perhaps for an Announcement, an Answer to the Riddle. It could be we have another half brother or a favored nephew to add to our basketful of princes. One more for the merry dogfight when Ywein dies!" Dewi sensed a thread of unease in the poet's amusement.

Llywarch Prydyt y Moch shrugged. "Squabblers all! I throw my lot in with the eldest. Ywein Gwynet long ago named Hywel as king to succeed him. Why should he unsay that promise?" The poet narrowed his gaze in a chilling change of mood and prodded Elisy with his foot. "Go repeating after me in the stable or the kitchen, puppy, and I will cheerfully wring your neck."

Burly Razo appeared in a doorway close by. He wiped the last drops of ale from his beard and with a jerk of his head called the boys from the wall. "Round up all them blessed hounds again, you two, and see they're shut fast. New orders is no dogs or brats underfoot out here."

Llywarch watched with a deepening frown as Elisy and Dewi called the hounds out of barrack and hall and dragged more up out of the kitchen. Quietly, armed men —Hywel's, not Iorwerth's—were deployed in doorways. Hywel's foster brothers, the seven sons of Cadifor, leaned on their swords not far from the great gate and now and then played at practicing together with their blades. Elisy, whose sense of self-preservation was highly developed, took the first opportunity to join the dogs in the warm safety of the kennel. The Poet of the Pigs drew back into an angle between the walls and chewed unhappily at his lip.

Dewi, earnestly playing his part, had chased two hounds still very much puppies up the tower from the hall. A darkly handsome man in rich blue and scarlet drew back in annoyance as the hounds bounded by on the narrow stair. They burst in upon the ladies and children sitting at breakfast in a tapestry-hung chamber, where furs were strewn on the rushes that covered the floor, and wooden bowls were filled from a silver tureen with a silver ladle. The little company was so cheered by the dogs' antics that they promised to keep them fast indoors if Dewi would stop staring and close the door as he went out. The children eyed him as if they were disappointed that he did not tear his hair and shout or fall into a fit or trance as a madman should.

On his way down, Dewi came to a window on the stair as the little cavalcade of riders rode over the shoulder of the hill and slowed before the gate. He saw that they laughed at some remark from the tall, flaxen-haired young man at their head, who kneed his horse, making him rear and strike with his hoofs at the gate.

"Prince Iorwerth! If there is a password, I do not know it! This crew of mine have a great thirst and are impatient. Must I break down your gate, or will you open?"

As the gate creaked open, Dewi watched the tall, blond man curiously. Taller than the others, and fairer, with a long merry face and sharp blue eyes, hair curly and flaxen, he must be the one called Madauc. Broad-chested, long-waisted, long-legged, he rode easily and held himself proudly as his horse lunged up the cobbled way into the castle Dolwydlan. He laughed, but the laughter died as swiftly as it rose.

Behind Madauc, the great gate rumbled shut in the startled faces of his followers. His horse was surrounded.

3
Escape

The most important thing was to get back, to undo the nightmare, to find the thing in himself that had drawn him through some crack in time and space into the kingdom of Gwynet in northern Wales of the twelfth century. It was not the "Dark Ages" after all, but a strange and frightening time when brutality and chivalry rode the same horse; when Gwynet stubbornly held its own against the English King Henry, whose kingdom stretched from England south to the Pyrenees—the Henry who in anger at his defeat at Rudlan had ordered the blinding of his Welsh hostages, the princes Cadwallawn and Kynwric, before sending them back to their father Ywein. The year was 1170. That much Dewi had gleaned, but it meant very little to him, except that somewhere, somehow, he had lost eight hundred years, and he wanted desperately to have them safely behind him once again.

He lay in the close darkness, warmed by Elisy on the one side and Mailcun on the other. The hound had crept close by cautious stages, as if he were torn with knowing it was Dewi and yet not Dewi, but in the end could not care so long as there was warmth and a kind hand. Elisy trembled slightly, as if he were a small leaf shaken by some wind of a dream that still whirled around the morning's violence. Dewi closed his eyes and listened to the night, but sleep and dreams hung out of reach. The vague, confused notion he had that somehow two dreams, two wishes, had gotten crossed convinced him that what he had to do was undream it all, dream it wasn't so, wind time back up. But sleeplessness held dreams away, and even awake he could not keep hold of one single self. His mind wandered, drifted into muddle. *What is my own dog's name? Not this one. Not Mailcun. Mine.* His father's face was blurred, and Mr. Trumbull, his Latin teacher, looked at him with the cold eyes of the dark man on the tower stair. *I have to get back.* He felt the old daydream—the one about an adventurous life where every tomorrow held its own surprise—blow away in a black wind that took his childhood with it. All he wanted was to be safe.

"Safe"—even the word shifted underfoot. One man's safety meant another's danger. Since morning Hywel had been safe from Madauc. The trap had been sprung. On the high stair Hywel had watched calmly, and Iorwerth had wrung his hands. Madauc's men outside the gate had been silenced by the archers on the ramparts before they understood their danger, and the dreadful game in the courtyard played itself out unhindered. Unhorsed, Madauc had managed to get the wall at his back, but Cadifor's sons, small men, quick and wiry, with soldiers waiting behind, were too many for him. Tired and hurt, he was brought down at last, like the wounded hart torn by the hounds while the hunter watches.

"No more, no more!"

The cry was Iorwerth's. The kinder-hearted, moon-faced prince had turned his eyes away at first, reluctant to watch, even though he had given in to Hywel's arguments. If their father in his dotage meant to set a young upstart before his eldest son, why then Hywel must defend himself against this whim of an old man's fevered, childish mind. But there was something about the young man . . . not the agility and the singing sword that taught a dozen knights and soldiers caution, but the desperate gallantry, the laugh and brave taunting insults that echoed too closely the death of Rien. Iorwerth's heart misgave him. Rien, the well-beloved, laughing, the sun on his flaxen curls, glinting off his flashing sword. Rien dead in Iorwerth's own arms. What if this lad *were* Ywein's son? Or Rien's? "No more," Iorwerth said more quietly. "Not here. Not within my gates."

In that moment the soldiers and Hywel's knights drew back, hesitating while the princes wrangled. Madauc, bloodied, breathless, leaned against the wall and then slid down it, crumpling like a child who fights off sleep but at last tumbles into it headlong.

Prince Hywel, his strong features flushed with anger, had put a hand to his own sword and started down the stair when, quick as an adder in the grass, Llywarch Prydyt y Moch slipped through the ring of hurt and wearied men to kneel beside Madauc, dagger drawn, his cat's eyes gleaming. He dragged Madauc's head up so that it rested against his own shoulder. The autumn sunshine lay in a bright pool around them.

"Shall I make an end of him for you, my lord?"

Prince Hywel froze. The moment hung motionless in the air, and all the watchers save Dewi at his high window knew or guessed what had drained the color from Hywel's face. The echo that so pained Iorwerth's kindly heart had pierced his, too, like a dagger blow that comes unlooked for. A drawn and dear face had rested just so against Iorwerth's shoulder in a sunny courtyard of the castle of Caer

Vyrdin. Rien. So long ago. This Madauc would have been a prattling youngster then . . .

"Put up your blade, Prydyt y Moch." Hywel forced the words out, his voice grating. "This is Iorwerth's ground. The life is his to spare, if so he wills." Even as he spoke, discontentment erased the tenderness that had dimmed his arrogance. "Perhaps I will let you kill him later," he said, and turned on his heel.

Dewi shuddered, remembering. Trapped on the inner stair when the princes retreated afterward to the hall, he heard it all: the shouting and the strange, brutal mercy the brothers settled on at last. Fearing their father's wrath and Madauc's vengeance if he ever again had the *teulu* at his back, fearing for their own lands and power, they did not dare retreat. The affair had carried too far. In the end it was Prydyt y Moch who reminded them how King Ywein had dealt with his nephew Guneda, him of the dangerous and overreaching ambition; and how Henry of England had served two of their brothers. A blind man, he said smoothly, could be a monk, perhaps, but little else. Ywein would soon be dead, and safety could be bought without murder. Hywel had stared at his poet-courtier as if he saw a stranger or a devil behind the familiar face. But then in a strangled voice he had said, "See to it, then."

Mailcun whimpered softly. Dewi came awake with a start. He had not slept, but the faint sound of voices that buzzed in the low room had for a long while hung at the farthest edge of hearing. He raised his head to listen, thinking for a moment that it might be guards talking outside the kennel door, but the voices were oddly distant and hollow and seemed to have their source more in the direction of the far corner of the kennel. The stone wall of the lesser tower met the outer castle wall there, and since there was no walkway on that stretch of rampart and a sheer drop below it, the voices were a puzzle. Dewi crawled toward them, clambering over sleeping dogs, and found that the murmurings issued from the mouth of a deep and narrow slit at the base of the wall. In the days before the addition of the kennels, it must have served as a ventilating shaft to the dungeons below. They had taken Madauc to some such place.

Far below, a small, glowing hole in the darkness wavered, disappeared, and then grew bright again: a lantern. And a dark figure that moved across the dungeon, obscuring the light from time to time. Words were exchanged, but they were as indistinguishable and the voices as unrecognizable as the moving shadows. Dewi sat back on his heels. Whatever was going on, he wanted none of it. He wanted only to shut his eyes and ears to it, to this place, to this time.

Elisy rolled over in his sleep. The dogs twitched and sighed and chased elusive foxes in their dreams, and Dewi crawled back among them to stretch out and try again to sleep. But the voices crept after him and into his imaginings. *No. Think about the way back. Across time and the wide sea.* He frowned, trying to remember, but his heart was drawn back again, swinging like a heavy pendulum toward that other sea dreamer shut up below. Madauc. What had Llywarch said of him? A dreamer of the land to the west? Dewi shivered with the cold. *Cat-sly Llywarch, he was the cold one, the deadly one. Prince Hywel at least had anger and some pity in him. Not Prydyt y Moch.* But why had the Poet of the Pigs, as they called him, looked so strangely at the silver pendant and then made as if it were nothing? Dewi felt for the medallion at his breast. Warm and heavy, it seemed heavier yet when he turned his mind to it. It pulled at him, as if the winged shape would draw him with it through the shining circle. Was it a winged man or a sea bird? *A sea gull? Madauc's ensign, the white gull on the blue ground.* It had been the same clean-winged, wheeling shape!

Dewi pushed the peg back into place and listened for a moment at the hole in the kennel door. He had gotten out without waking the younger boy, but Mailcun was at the door with a soft, begging whine. Dewi thrust his arm through the little wicket opening to rub the dog behind the ears. "You stay, now. And hush that." The hound was quiet. Dewi turned to scan the courtyard.

A paring of a moon rode high over the cobbled yard, faintly lighting the castle keep and most of the courtyard itself, leaving in deep shadow the edge where Dewi stood. The shadow lay wide along the kennel wall and more narrowly by the stables and the lower tower. It was through the second of the doors along the tower wall that Llywarch and the soldiers had disappeared with Madauc. The first was the entrance to the guardroom and the upper stair. Neither had an outer door, but there would be stout doors within. Still, he meant to find the downward stair and the door to that deep room, if it were possible. What help listening at a door might be, he could not have said. He was drawn more by the winged figure, by the hunger to know what it might mean, than by any wild hope of aiding the blind and helpless prisoner. Perhaps Iorwerth had crept down to speak with him. Perhaps. Or Father Gwillim.

The shadows made a safe corridor between wall and moonlight. Dewi reached the first tower door easily, reached across to touch the wall beyond, and moved quickly to the second door, an invisible hole in the blackness. Once inside, he moved cautiously, both hands fingering along the wall, feeling one step forward at a time with an outstretched foot. Coming to the passage end and the stair, he stopped to listen; but the voices had left off. In the stillness he stooped to feel along the step and, finding that the next one down was wedge-shaped, kept close to the wall as he descended. The stairway was circular and had neither a rail nor any sort of handhold on the smooth stone core at the center where each step narrowed to nothing. Dewi had crept no farther than the first eight or ten steps when he was sent scrambling back the way he had come by the groan of hinges coaxed to quietness and the rumble of wood on stone. The door below had opened, and yellow beams from a half-shaded lantern danced upward around the circling walls. Shuffling, scuffling sounds, low voices, and heavy breathing rustled far below, magnified by the narrowness of the place and by Dewi's straining ears. He retreated as a cloaked and hooded figure climbed into sight, humping up the steps a little like a stout three-legged dog, the lantern held in one hand, with the other making an extra foot for the high-stepped stair. Dewi turned and fled along the passage and out through the door into the courtyard, to lean breathless against the wall.

"Hsst!"

Dewi heard the agitated whisper and held his breath in an attempt to quiet the beating of his heart, which drummed so loudly that it seemed impossible the whisperer and the soldiers sleeping not twenty feet away did not hear it.

"Hsst! Oh, quickly! I heard a small something . . . no, not a rat's scurry . . . a little footstep. Ah, holy Blessed Illtud, help us!"

Dewi peered in again at the doorway, but the light had been extinguished. Whoever had spoken had recovered quickly from alarm, and Dewi no sooner drew back than someone padded quickly past him and back again, making soft, fussing noises that were somehow familiar. The near encounter was so close that he had a clear impression of a short, bent, bustling shape he should have known, and he hurried as far as the guardroom passage, to take uneasy shelter there. The soldiers snored behind their door, and outside, footsteps shuffled awkwardly. The conspirators, if that was what they were, were not so cautious as their lookout. Three figures moved openly across the moonlit cobbles in a straight line for the gate. The tallest was supported by the other two.

Madauc! But who were the others? And why? And why, if they were friends come to free him, did they take so little care? Surely they would be seen. Dewi followed, keeping to the shadows. Where were the guards, the night watch?

The door in the great gate stood open, and no sentry was in sight. Fearing that something was very wrong, Dewi hesitated. The uneasy sense that the scene was being watched, that even he was watched, made him falter. Something, a slight movement, drew his attention up the sweep of the outer tower stair to the doorway of Iorwerth's hall. There was no mistaking the man who stood there, caring little whether he stood in light or shadow. The figure, the round moon-face were Iorwerth's. So then he knew! Before he was quite aware of it, a decision at once his own and not his own sent Dewi running across that same stretch of moonlight to the gate. He was through, and it had closed behind him.

"Dewi? Thank the holy saints for luck! We should have thought of him before, my friend." A short, hooded figure detached itself from a tree across the road and moved into the shadow of the castle wall, leading a pony along behind it.

"Father?" Dewi's whisper was almost a croak. Alarm stiffened him, as it had that morning with Elisy. How could he recognize someone he had never seen? The hood slipped down, and he saw that it was the old priest, a most unlikely and agitated conspirator.

"Indeed, my son, you come most happily for us." Father Gwillim's voice trembled. "Prince Iorwerth wishes Lord Madauc safe away from further harm, and yet he does not choose openly to oppose his brother. This morning's work has been a sad harbinger of what may come if Prince Hywel should be challenged after Ywein Gwynet dies. Brother against brother. . . . But I must not gabble you a sermon here." The old man turned in the darkness to his companion. "It is better that Dewi go than you or I. No duty will be broken, then, neither his nor ours, for Dewi was to be sent to Bangor in the spring, and what is a winter more or less?"

"Bangor?"

The old priest missed the bewilderment in Dewi's question. "Ah, not at once. Your studies still must wait, child. Our young friend the lord Madauc cannot travel so far, and you must see him safely to the holy hermit Gruffyt's chapel on the east bank of the Conwy in Rhos. He is a skillful healer, and though we have done our best, that is what is needed now."

"I know old Gruffyt." Madauc's voice was shaky, but it still held a hint of laughter. "A rascal grown holy! But come, leave off your talking and help me mount. I can point the way to the boy as we go. A mile or three downstream there is a way north across the hills that will keep us safe away from roads."

They were an awkward length of time getting him onto the pony. When it was accomplished, the old man whispered hurriedly, "When you are well enough again, send word with Dewi to the Bishop of Bangor, and he will surely grant you sanctuary with the good brothers of some hospitable monastery." There was a catch in the old priest's voice. "I am sorry, my son. I know quite well it is a life you would never have chosen."

"But the sword and the sea are not for a blind man? I know." The low voice was slurred, too tired for bitterness. "Come. I fear I cannot ride for long, and I want the hills around me."

Just as the shadow that was Father Gwillim faded toward the gate, the second dark, hooded figure moved out from the wall to stand at the pony's head, a hand on the bridle, and speak with a strange intentness. "You are no monk, my lord, to sit and blindly count your fingers in a cloister garden. Why should a blind man not go on pilgrimage? I am bard and seer, my lord, and I lay this penance upon you for so long as Hywel is set against you: keep the boy by you, and *go on pilgrimage.*"

The drawling speech had a strange pointedness to it, as much plea as warning; but all Dewi knew was that the voice was Llywarch's, and it seemed unbearable that mocking threats should follow so hard upon betrayal and injury. He did not wonder what doubleness must have prompted the Poet of the Pigs to aid Iorwerth in thwarting Hywel. All the anger and bewilderment of the past twenty hours welled up in him, and he threw himself at Llywarch in a fury, striking him such a solid blow that the poet reeled and stumbled.

"Fair enough," Llywarch breathed. He picked himself up. "Fair enough for a lad who doesn't know what he's fallen into. I suppose I owed you that."

And, catlike, he was gone. A heavy oaken bar groaned into place, fastening Dolwydlan against the night. Shaking, fighting back tears, Dewi groped for the pony's reins and moved in a slow daze onto the moonlit road. Nothing. He understood nothing. Even this wild day's world was snatched away from him. He understood nothing and felt only that he walked deeper into nightmare. *The blind leading the blind, in truth.* He almost laughed as he stumbled on the uneven track and caught himself.

"Are you all right, boy?" The voice was soft and tired.

"Yes."

Yes. Strangely, yes.

4
Adrift

In the first thin light Dewi crawled from the warm nest in the tangled thicket to see what had alarmed the pony. Something had set it stamping and crashing around the tree where it was tied. Dismayed, Dewi saw that a long wallet-shaped bag he had missed seeing in the darkness had worked loose from the thongs that bound it to the saddle, to drag upon the ground and twist around the pony's near hind foot. It was untangled in a moment, but the damage had been done. The provisions it contained were sadly trampled: oatcake and peasecake reduced to bits and crumbs, an egg pie squashed. At least the cold roast mutton and a roll of clean linen, Dewi supposed, with a qualm, to be bandages, had been wrapped separately and were in better shape.

Fortunately, too, Father Gwillim had tied the leather bottle of mead securely at the front of the saddle, and Dewi washed down a hasty breakfast of crumbs and meat with a long swallow of the honey liquor. He almost retched. It was sickeningly sweet and strong and burned all the way down. The warmth that spread through him, though, was delicious in the dawn chill, but it made his head swim unpleasantly. He put the stopper back and broke off a piece of the pie to take with the bandages and the bottle to Madauc. The wounded man had slept only fitfully in the long hours—two? three?—since they had taken cover above the river road. Madauc had told him where, after the second small cluster of farm buildings beyond Dolwydlan, to look for the upward path; but its roughness and the pony's lunging uphill gait had jarred him cruelly. He was a big man, and when he fell in dismounting, Dewi had despaired of getting him to the shelter of the nearby scrub trees. Somehow they managed. But in that, too, damage had been done. Now in the half-light Dewi could see the pain in the drawn face below the bandaged eyes, and it was with a shiver that he undid the fastenings of the heavy cloak and unpinned the brooch securing the loose linen garment underneath. One of the priest's old surplices, it looked like: slit down the front so that it would not bind across the shoulders of the larger man. As he loosened it, Dewi had to stifle an urge to shut his eyes. He did not know what to expect. It was almost as if he had never seen worse than a nosebleed or bloody knuckles in a schoolyard fight. (Where had that been?) Knowing there was no one to help made it easier, and he saw with relief that someone had skillfully bound up the more serious hurts. The difficulty was that the heavy bandage around the man's waist had slipped, and one side was darkly stained with blood. *Fold the first triangular bandage to make a band four inches wide, and then fold from one end, making a firm pad. If bound securely against the wound, the pad will exert the necessary pressure. . .* .The lesson echoed from a corner of his memory as obscure as that which knew Father Gwillim in the dark and called Elisy and Mailcun by name.

Mailcun. The dog lay still, alert and watching, as if he understood and approved. Who had loosed him, Dewi could not be sure, but he had come lolloping, panting after them as they reached the road along the stream below Dolwydlan. Iorwerth's most prized hound? Father Gwillim would not have dared to send him; no more would the pig-poet, unless Iorwerth. . . . But, runaway or prince's blessing, he was welcome. Dewi wondered if he had ever been so happy as when the dog's warm muzzle pressed into his hand in greeting.

The boy's fingers moved more surely than his thoughts, and the ugly wound was dressed again. Madauc had groaned when the thin arm slid the outer bandage under the small of his back, and he lay breathing in a quick and shallow rhythm.

"Who are you, boy?" he whispered. "And why does Llywarch bid me keep you by me?"

A lark pealed its chain of sweet morning notes overhead. The pony snuffled and cropped at the grass. Dewi fastened the cloak and wrapped its folds securely around his charge.

"I don't know," he answered at last, almost matter-of-factly. "Sometimes it seems I'm the Dewi they sent to Dolwydlan when my mother died of grieving for my father. Sometimes I know I've come out of another time and a faraway place. And sometimes both. But it is harder all the time to remember that other place." He frowned. "I can't explain it, unless it's that I'm crazy."

The injured man seemed only to have heard a part of what Dewi said. He raised his hand to touch the boy's arm and confided in a ragged whisper, "I am someone and no one, too. But that won't make us brothers, will it? Foster brothers, perhaps. There will be too much blood between blood brothers . . ."

He coughed, and the boy helped him raise his head a little to drink from the bottle. It seemed to steady him, and there was more color in his cheeks. "Have we come far?"

"Not three miles."

"Then it will be close on eight more to the hermit's."

Dewi guessed what Madauc was thinking. He could never ride so far. With a little help he had a bit of the pie and drank again, but afterward lay back exhausted.

"We must wait until tonight, then," Dewi said. "You'll feel stronger."

"Yes . . ." Madauc's attention drifted. His voice was thicker, a little slurred, when he spoke again. "What is the faraway place you are from, then?"

The boy hesitated. He found he did not want to put a name to what he remembered. *Ohio* would sound even more unreal spoken to the open air than its image looked in his memory. It shifted and shimmered, a shattered reflection in a troubled pool. "No place you ever heard of," he answered, trying to recapture it for himself. "It's very far away, thousands of miles across the ocean. I suppose it would be mostly forest now. But it doesn't matter. No one will find it for hundreds of years. There was a river. I do remember that. We went upriver most summers. My uncle had a boat when I was small, and he took me on the river once. But then he sold his river land and the boat because they took more looking after than they were worth, he said."

"What kind of boat?"

"Oh, an ordinary dinghy sort of rowboat. I . . ."

But the thick, unsteady voice went on. "We never did build *Gwennan Gorn,* did we? D'you remember how we raced around th' island, first boat to be captain? How I was first, with you coming furious after, and how Llywarch stove a hole in his coracle and sank off Rat Island?"

Llywarch again.

Madauc's hand gripped Dewi's arm with surprising strength, and he struggled to raise himself. "You've not forgot what you swore? We will build *Gwennan Gorn?* And sail out over the sea's edge? You've not forgot . . . ?"

"No, no." Frightened, Dewi soothed him and tried to push him down. "Tomorrow. We can begin tomorrow." *Whatever Gwennan Gorn might be.* "I promise."

It seemed to satisfy. Madauc lay back weakly, but kept

his grip on Dewi's arm. "You see," he whispered desperately, moving his head from side to side as if he searched for something, "there will be gold there, and silver, and rivers of pearls. Mountains of adamant and beryl and ruby. I see them. I shall bring more riches to Gwynet than Henry of England has, and my brothers will fight among themselves which will be my friend. My brother . . ."

Dewi gave him more of the mead to drink and sat beside him, seeing with despair how the fever took hold. Eight miles might as well be eight hundred.

"Ithil?" The word was a whisper. "Ithil?" It seemed to be a name.

"Yes, what is it?" Dewi leaned close.

"Nothing." The hand fell away from his arm and then reached up to fumble at the cord around Dewi's neck. Dragging the medallion free of the boy's tunic, Madauc gripped it, running a thumb along the lines of the winged figure. "You have it still. It is good you've come back, Ithil. You'll not . . ."

"No, I won't go away. Don't worry. But you'd better sleep, or we won't be able to—" He broke off. Madauc had already fallen into sleep.

Ithil. Madauc had mistaken him for someone named Ithil, and the sea bird had assured him of it. Ithil . . . *who never returned from an embassy to France. Ambushed by King Henry's men. My father, Ithil.*

But the sense of doubleness was somehow less troubling. For each new remembering, a fragment of that other past slipped beyond his reach, yet this exchange no longer seemed so frightening. *You have a center all your own,* he thought, *but the rest of what you are comes from touching what's around you: people and places, even things. Maybe the two of us have only switched centers, and after a bit we'll grow fast into where we are and not remember at all.* There was both relief and sadness in thinking so.

At the same time, it occurred to the boy that there were precautions he should take before sunup. He moved quickly and quietly about them, picketing the pony in a small clearing well away from the narrow hill track and gathering brush to screen the other grassy hollow deep in the thicket where Madauc lay. Leaving Mailcun to stand guard, he back-tracked and searched out a sheltered place overlooking the valley road from Dolwydlan. During the early morning he made a number of trips from this lookout to see that Madauc still slept, for he was afraid of what might happen if the man woke to find himself alone in his darkness.

The vigil above the road had its reward when, in the hour before noon, a large body of horsemen approached from the direction of the castle, moving briskly. A banner of a red dragon on a blue ground fluttered in the breeze of their going. But did Prince Hywel know of Madauc's escape? An answer came hard upon the silent question, for two riders turned off and up the hill path, climbing without haste, searching the trail and its borders for any sign of the fugitives. They passed within yards of Dewi's hiding place among the rocks.

Hywel was a careful man. The road down the Lledr and north along the river Conwy was the better road, but the longer way. He would send scouts, like these, onto every northbound trail. In a way the fugitives were safer than if they could have kept to their road, for they must have gone at a snail's pace, with every likelihood of being overtaken before they gained the hermit Gruffyt's chapel.

Crumbled oatcake, pie, and water from a small stream nearby made both Dewi's and Mailcun's midday and evening meals. The boy saved the mead and what was left of the pie and mutton. Evening wore into night, and though the fever passed at sundown, Madauc slept like a dead man, and Dewi could not rouse him.

* * *

Two hours before dawn Dewi awoke to find himself covered by a fold of the warm cloak and Madauc sitting beside him, his back to a young tree. He gnawed at the mutton bone in the dark and sounded almost cheerful.

"A pity it was such a small bottle, Dewi, lad. There's not a drop left for you, nor a shred of meat for your long-eared friend. He must content himself with a well-polished bone."

At the news of Hywel's passing, Madauc frowned. "I wonder why he himself should hurry north. If he was for Aberffraw, he would be taking the western road. Damnation! A few promises of silver and brother Hywel will have half the vale a-watch."

"*Is* he your brother, then?" Dewi had not believed it could be true.

"Half brother. Does that disturb you so, boy?" The voice in the dark held a wry amusement. "It's said by some that Ywein's had five wives and fathered twenty sons, and that would leave more than me unaccounted for! I doubt the truth will ever be opened up, for the old man's heart is like a miser's dark cupboard: bound around with chains and padlocks. He admits only to two wives—the old queen and her who came after—and their sons are not likely to call me brother so long as our father will not name me son." Madauc's tone was dry, but his detachment was not very convincing. "Ywein Gwynet in his old age is as hard a man as ever he was. Long years ago he turned against my mother—why, she never knew—and denying he had ever wed her, took her sons from her: my own brothers Kynan and Rien and Rhirid. Rien he loved, but he imprisoned Kynan and banished Rhirid to our mother's father's lands in Ireland. I was not born till after."

There was a pause, then, bitterly, "She's been dead these ten years now, but it seems that Ywein hates her memory still too much to bruise his pride by claiming me. It's the wife who came after—our dear Queen Cristin—who's to thank for that, I'm thinking." He sighed, then moved impatiently. "But enough of old envies! Come, finish this mangled pie. We must be off."

Before dawn they came down into the shadows of the valley of the Llugwy and forded the stony stream, following on the far side past the watersmeet where it joined the Conwy. In this way they avoided bridge and houses and came at an hour before travelers were abroad to the north road where it marched between the river and steep wooded hills. Madauc was pale and tired, but he would not stop.

"There is a place this side of Trefriw . . . another mile perhaps. We must be across the river before Trefriw. I have friends there, but Hywel will have thought of that, and they will be watched. You must tell me when we come to the stretch where the river bends in again toward the road. There will be a farmhouse."

It was there, a long, low building with a blind back turned to the road.

"There will be a boat, I think. Leave the dog with me and see if there is a boat."

Dewi returned to the road to say that, though there was no proper boat, he had seen a strange rounded cockleshell of a thing propped upended on a paddle. "Yes, it's big enough." He sounded doubtful. "It's near as long as you are tall, and it has three strong thwarts."

"What more would you be needing on a river?" Madauc was sharp in his impatience. With Dewi's help he dismounted and then ordered the boy onto the pony's back. He drew the hood of the cloak down to shadow his face, and from the unsteadiness of his gait as he walked, guided by a hand on the pony's withers and the dog at his knee, they would have seemed to any watcher only a farm lad and an elderly priest. Once they had gained the riverbank, Madauc sat himself down and sent Dewi off to find the farmer. "He should be in his dairy by now. Tell him we wish to borrow his coracle, and you will leave your pony with him as our bond. Say we go to—to Degannwy." His breath came unevenly. The short walk had left him trembling.

The arrangement was easily made, and in a few moments Dewi was back and dragging the odd hide-covered boat into the water. The farmer came behind "to hand the good father in," for which Dewi was thankful; and if the farmer wondered at the girth of the good father's arm, he said nothing. Mailcun leaped in easily after them.

"Mind the Arw rocks!" the farmer called after as they drifted out into the current, moving northward under the dark climbing woods of the west shore until the river bent once more toward the gentler eastern hills and the dawn.

Dewi dipped the paddle nervously, trying to keep to the middle of the stream, but the strange craft did not answer like a canoe. It rocked alarmingly, turned half circle, and drifted on stern first. Mailcun whimpered softly.

"What do I do? Where are the rocks he meant?" Madauc's assurance had swept Dewi this far, but now the absurdity and danger of a blind man and a hound and a lost boy drifting northward willy-nilly swept over and nearly drowned him. "How will I know when we come to where we're going? It won't steer. I'll never get us to shore again!"

"So I see." There was a hint of smothered laughter in the low remark. "You must not stroke off to the side so. Once more, perhaps, to bring yourself back around . . . good. Now, kneel so that you can reach directly forward and pull the stroke toward you. Ah, not so deep! Without my weight behind, that stroke would have had you in head first. Yes, good. And it takes but a little pull to the right or left well after the middle of the stroke."

Dewi's shoulders began to ache, but though he could not catch the rhythm quite, he found that he could change direction easily enough. Still, he worried about the rocks. He asked again.

"We do not go as far as the Arw rocks, only to the shore opposite Trefriw. I will tell you where. And after that, Dewi ap Ithil? Why, after that there is the building of *Gwennan Gorn* and the voyage over the sea's edge!"

Dewi turned to look over his shoulder, dismayed at this echo of yesterday's disordered dreamings; but though Madauc looked very ill, he did not seem fevered. To Dewi's astonishment he even laughed, and the dark hood slid back.

"I will tell you where," he had said.

Dewi almost dropped the paddle. The sun was up, the bandage was gone, and Madauc's eyes gleamed as blue as sky and water.

5

The Winged Man

It had been a trick, Llywarch's wild gamble, as Dewi was later to learn. But though Madauc's eyes were—marvel of marvels!—unhurt, his "after that" was not to come as soon as he had hoped. Gruffyt, the hermit, thought it unlikely his patient would be fit to travel before Christmas, for the effort Madauc had willed himself to make in reaching safety had left him too weak to fight off fever and the inflammation of the lungs that followed it. In the first week the aged hermit made no secret of his concern, but under his care the danger slowly passed. To Madauc he said, "Rest easy. Do not hurry yourself. Time is what you must have, and you should be safe enough in this place even if Prince Hywel should come to hear of it. He forces his will in most things, but has never dragged a man from a church. Indeed, I sometimes wonder why, but he has always respected the law of sanctuary." The old man smiled. "By that law you are under my rule now, and my rule is: peace and quiet."

The hermit's periodic disappearances from his chapel cell by the river were thought nothing unusual by the occasional villager who came to trade eggs or flour for the honey from Gruffyt's hives, and so his frequent retreats to the long-deserted church in the wooded hills above the chapel excited no notice.

These weeks of Madauc's recovery would have been a pleasant time for Dewi if he could have shaken free of that blankness that settled like a white fog over his mind each time he attempted to reason his way through the confusion of selves and times and places that could turn even the smallest and homeliest of things into ambush and alarm. The river Conwy glimpsed through the trees, the crinkled black caps of mushrooms growing in the deserted churchyard, the tales of kings and saints and heroes old Gruffyt recited in a singsong whisper as he and the boy watched through the long evenings, sitting beside a glowing brazier in the derelict church—all of these things were familiar. Or were they? Each time, the question came hard upon the recognition, and what had seemed so reassuring dimmed to an uncertain echo. Was it an echo of someone else's memory? That other boy, the other Dewi . . . Dave. Which was which? Perhaps . . . perhaps both were dreams. Perhaps. . . . The blankness always came as he gave himself to that swift, confusing stream of rushing thought.

Another time, waking in the middle night to hear the distant horn of a car, he smelt the fragrance of the rambler rose that climbed beside his bedroom window and heard Brownie in the garage, yapping in sharp frustration at a tomcat caterwauling in a nearby garden. The thought came: *I ought to shut him up.* If the Abernethys complained again, his father might carry out the threat to send the terrier off to Uncle Jim, at the farm. He struggled to open his eyes, but his eyelids were heavy, weighted, slow to answer, as if between the impulse and the response an age slid by. The wailing and barking faded to a muffled clamor as he awoke to see the moonlit room, to feel the crisp smoothness of clean sheets, to try to swing his legs over the bed's edge and grope for the slippers that should be there.

But the other had wakened with him. While Dewi watched, willing his heavy self to move, the now-Dave jerked with alarm. Throwing off the covers, he lunged from the bed and backed stumbling toward the window, pressing nervously at the corners of his eyes, trying desperately to make out the dim, sleep-numbed shape on the bed, breathing with the shallow, frantic rapidity of a small, threatened animal. "*You leave me be!*" he hissed.

And Dewi had fallen awake, out of the dream into the damp, chill darkness of the church, the rough linen of the bracken-filled pallet damp under his cheek. For all the sick sense of the lost chance of regaining the security of the future, of forcing some exchange with the boy whose dreams had crossed with his, shunting each to new realities—for all this, and the salt taste of tears, he had felt a queer, wild pang of relief.

The days were full despite their quiet sameness. There were visits to the farm close by for eggs and milk and curd cheese, and forays down to the river to barter with the cor-

acle men for fish and for news of the world beyond the province of Rhos. In the afternoons, while Madauc slept, Father Gruffyt hitched up his robes and went berry-picking with Dewi in the bramble-grown churchyard, or wandered in the wood, discoursing on the virtues and perils of the autumn varieties of mushroom. The gentle old man knew every flower and herb, every wild creature in the wood; and in the pleasure of having a curious boy to teach —a boy so oddly ignorant of much that was common knowledge—old Gruffyt lost some of the shyness that had grown upon him in his long retirement.

Dewi began to feel his own roots stretching out, taking hold in this time and place, the present reaching, mercifully, like green and spreading ivy, to cover the cracks in the wall that had been growing between present and future. The sense of things newly met, of the days' freedom, was exhilarating and, with the hovering possibility of danger—however remote at the moment—kept his mind from picking at the frayed and puzzling threads of other realities.

One day early in November, when the confidence between the old man and the boy had deepened beyond what is usual between age and youth, Gruffyt, groping for words to convey his premonition, confided to Dewi a worry that had grown as Madauc grew.

"He has changed—and not changed enough. Of course, young Madauc was scarce half your age when last I saw him; but I do not mean only that he has altered and grown to manhood. . . ." He rubbed his elbow in a by now familiar nervous gesture. "I saw him twice at Ywein's court at Aberffraw in Von. Twenty years ago, it must have been. His mother brought him, hoping that Ywein would see what a goodly lad he was and take an interest in him, but each time they were turned away. He seemed a happy lad, despite that, and full of lively curiosity. . . ."

The old man went on slowly, painfully. "It is little wonder that he is changed. So have we all, perhaps myself more than most. I was an old soldier in those days, but there came at last a time when I lost the stomach for it. Oh" —he met Dewi's surprise with a wry amusement—"oh yes, once I was as wild and bloody as any. But those were years to dismay many hard hearts. Prince Rien died when we drove the Normans from the southern kingdoms of Wales, and many thousands in Wales and England perished with a sickness some say the holy Crusaders brought out of the East. War and disease and the worm that eats at the heart! King Ywein imprisoned his son Kynan, Madauc's eldest brother, saying he schemed to gain the crown. War was everywhere: kinsman against kinsman, neighbor against neighbor, Gwynet with the kingdoms of Powys and Ceredigion, and Ywein with his own brother Cadwaladr. Soldiers like myself were leaves blown here and there by the windy anger of princes. But one day, on a bloody field in Gwent it was, I had a vision: a terrible vision where the battle stood still and the din was swept away on a red wind. I saw that every tree, every stone and flower bled—the very heart of the world bled with each blow I had struck, and I saw that it was our own hearts we devoured so hungrily." The old man rose and paced back and forth in his agitation. "When the vision passed, I broke my sword upon a stone and walked away. And now is Lord Madauc's chance to walk away. But he will not."

"But he means to be doing just that! He talks of nothing else but making some special kind of boat and sailing to the lands the old tales tell of."

"No, no." The old man shook his head. "His dreams are set in no new world. His heart is too much here. He dreams of winning fame and wealth, and with them power. He is like the child who cries, 'I will show them!' It is 'to show them' that he has served his father so well—too well—and won only as far as the rank of *penteulu*. The old hurt bites deeper with time. I would dissuade him from this voyage with which he frets himself. Where is he to build this boat? And what crew will he find but outlaws? Even if he should succeed, it will bring him no peace. It cannot undo a single moment of all those he counts as lost, and I am thinking the king cannot live to see it accomplished."

Dewi was silent. He remembered Madauc's feverish ramblings and had himself held some of these same doubts. But enthusiasm for the venture had grown on him and now outweighed the misgivings. The hermit's words drifted in the current of his thoughts and turned in a slow swirl. *It cannot undo a single moment of all those he counts as lost.* But if Madauc could look for one thing and find something else? Dewi could not think what it was he himself hoped to find across the sea. There had been something. . . . He took refuge in the present moment, bending to the task of skinning the rabbit for the evening's stew. Old Gruffyt watched him for a while and then put aside his uneasiness and returned to his patient.

"Ah, too much of peace and quiet have made Gruffyt an old woman!" Madauc said. "Once Gruffyt ap Morgan could outfight and outshoot any foot soldier in Britain, he was that skilled with the pike and the bow. But now he has grown as timid as a coney in its snug burrow. No, it is not quiet I need. Llywarch had the right of it. Do you remember? 'Go on pilgrimage,' he said, and that is what we shall be doing." He looked up at Dewi. "What is it now? That sour look would curdle milk."

"Llywarch. You . . . you should not trust that one so."

"I see. Or rather, I do not see. Why? Prydyt y Moch risked no life more than his own in all his playing at the villain. Even old Father Gwillim was fooled and did as he asked only because, good soul, he desired my escape. Why, Llywarch acted execution upon my eyes with such cold efficiency that brother Hywel himself turned away from the lamplight and the door and could not watch."

"Luckier for you than him!"

"Than Llywarch? What would you be meaning by that?"

Dewi reddened, but spoke defiantly. "I mean, if he couldn't have gotten away with it, he wouldn't have stopped at pretending. Out in that courtyard there was no chance of fooling anyone if Prince Hywel had told him yes, to go ahead and . . . and make an end of you. He just gambled he wouldn't be having to."

"And had he lost, he'd have gone through with it then?"

Madauc stared in surprise. Clearly it was a new thought. And then he laughed. "You may be right indeed, though I doubt it. Llywarch always loved a gamble. The greater the risk, the better. I would not much care to be at stake in his game again, though. He sails too near the wind and loses as often as he wins. I recall . . ." He broke off. "Tell me, Dewi ap Ithil: do you remember your father?"

Dewi hedged. "What's he to do with Llywarch?"

"Much. As much almost as I have, for we three were boys together. Like you, when my mother died, I was sent away—but south, to the island called Lund, to be horseboy to the lord of the island, Sir Jordan Marisco. The friends I found there were the first I had known: a scrawny brat who helped the pig keeper, and a lad a bit older than myself who was a shepherd."

"Llywarch and my . . . my father?" The word was heavy, a weight on his tongue, a stone to be rolled away. But once freed of it, he wondered at his hesitation.

"Just so. Ithil, Madauc, and Llywarch: the Three Great Voyagers of the Island of Britain, or so we dreamed. Boats and the sea were almost more than food to us, and we stole what hours we could to scour the island for caves and coves. Llywarch fell once, climbing a cliff, and broke his arm; and it angered his master the pig keeper, so that he beat poor Llywarch until he could no more carry a bucket with the good arm than with the bad." Madauc shook his head, remembering. "It was Llywarch's foolhardiness that led us to Diermit, the seer. That is, we believed he was a seer. *He* thought he was. But seer or no—and I think now he must have been only a poor mad Irish sailor—seer or no makes little matter. It happened one summer afternoon we had challenged each other to a race in our coracles, winner to be captain: and skimming down the eastern shore along the shadow of the cliffs and out around the long, rocky point, Ithil and I drew well ahead of Llywarch. We might have known he would try cutting ahead of us through the Devil's Gates. At full tide it is a narrow channel between the point and Rat Island, and when the tide is falling, the passage is truly dangerous. When he did not come out on the other side, we were sure he was drowned. He surely deserved to be, for it was a fool's trick. When the tide was low enough for us to pull our coracles onto a rock ledge and go peering into pools for his body, where did we find him but sitting safe in the mouth of a cave—a subterranean passage carved under the little island—safe and snug and listening to the wild sea tales of Diermit. High tales of shipwreck and a new land to the north beyond Ireland called Great Ireland, where Irishmen had settled; of Brendan's Isle, and Antillia where seven kings rule seven cities richer than Byzantium. He had seen the Fortunate Isles, he said, and Avallach with its magic fountains and birds singing in silver apple trees."

"But that's not true!"

Madauc grinned. "No. At least, I doubt the wonders, though I fear I swallowed 'em whole at the time. Don't you see, he gave our wishes shapes to move in. Of Antillia, he said, 'There is an island you must seek, for it is lost.' I can hear him yet, singing in his high, cracked whisper, 'Long ago it was found and lost again, and men have always said seeking will not find it; only chance. But this I do not believe.' And he made us swear by our hearts and his talisman that we would seek and find the lost island." Madauc reached up to touch a finger to Dewi's breast.

"This?" Dewi was startled. He pulled the silver disc out to look at it again. "This was your seer's talisman? Was that how you knew who I was?" As he fingered it, a wisp of memory drifted closer: a man—his father?—giving the silver circle and taking a small child's promise, a bewildering promise to seek what was lost.

"Diermit gave it to Ithil because he was oldest," Madauc explained. "He claimed it had been given him in Antillia and had great power. That was when we began to doubt his truth a little, it was so tall a tale. Later he admitted he had lied, but his 'truth' was stranger yet. He would have it that his father's grandfather had it off a drowned man washed ashore on Aran, off the west coast of Ireland: a dark-complexioned, strange-featured man with eyes as blue as harebells. The tale as Diermit told it was that the man and a woman were found lashed to a raft made of wreckage of their ship and that the woman was not dead when they were brought ashore. She was dressed in a gown of pearls, and was very beautiful, and over and over whispered words they could not understand. This frightened the islanders, and they wished to put her back into the sea. It was Diermit's father's grandfather who stopped them, for he had understood her whisperings, and he took her to his cottage, where she died."

"How could he have understood?"

Madauc smiled. "As men understand birds and beasts in tales of magic, I imagine. It seems the old man was a sailor and knew something of Gwynet and Little Britain and the Norselands, and he claimed the woman spoke her riddle in a tongue very like the Welsh. That made the tale more credible to his hearers, but how could folk from across the western sea chance to speak a tongue like ours, and we know nothing of them or their country? I am thinking the riddle must have been his own. Yet, it *is* strange; as dark as the western sea before the dawn. It sticks in the mind." He closed his eyes and recited softly:

"Man folds his wings
To tread the narrowing ring;
The serpent throned devours the circle
And himself.

"Winter's rule is violent,
Summer's song is silent,
The island of the apple trees
Is drowned in war.

"Unknown the oracle's round;
Yet if the lost be found,
And if the fallen spring again,
Then
Stones shall bruise the serpent's head
And summer's song be sung again."

Madauc smiled at Dewi's fascination as if he saw Ithil again, sitting cross-legged and starry-eyed among the rocks of Lund, while old Diermit spun his nets of dreams. In an ordinary tone, he said, "The old fellow grew wilder and stranger as the months wore on, and at times he was almost frightening. Yet we did believe him when he told us 'the sea bird will find a way.'" Madauc frowned slightly and avoided Dewi's eyes. "And so it has, after a fashion; for the land your father's tales have set you dreaming of is our same lost island. Six weeks west of the Islands of the Moon, so Diermit and the old tales said. Had you not stirred my remembering, the land to the west might have become no more than a pleasant, fading daydream. Chance has served us well."

"Chance?" Dewi twisted the pendant on its cord and closed his eyes against the strange memories that beat about him like white wings in the shadowy chancel of the crumbling church. Madauc, the dampness, and the sour smell of the pallets and mildewed clothing seemed far away, themselves a dream. The past-that-is-future swept over him like a breaker that crashes, sends the unwary swimmer sprawling, and ebbs away to leave him stunned and breathless on the shore. In that one moment, with an intensity almost too great to bear, he knew both his selves.

"No!" Shivering, he pulled the talisman on its cord from around his neck and thrust it at Madauc. "It was no accident. It *found* a way. It brought me here. Take it!"

The young man stared, puzzled by the boy's sudden revulsion. "Of course it didn't bring you. You brought *it*. Why, what ails you? You would like to know if the land you've thought and dreamed of does exist, wouldn't you? As I do? Why should Diermit's cracked riddles fright you? He was mad, child."

The circle that framed the silver sea bird's flight in the palm of Madauc's hand glistened, glinted as if the shape itself were an echo or shadow of some power it held within it to bring him circling through time. Ithil had given it to him, yes. But he had found it, too, in that far-off river cave. *Would* find it. Had not yet. No, had *and* would, for his *own* past was in the future now. How could that be? He remembered things that would not happen for eight hundred years! In a sudden illumination he saw that time was not a thread strung with happenings, separate and perfect, like polished stones. Was time itself a glinting circle, always whole but gleaming only where the moment's light glanced off it? The meaning of that soaring shape, free and yet bounded, eluded him. "The land I told you of?" he ventured. "I didn't dream it. Eight hundred years from now I lived there. And it was a boy who wanted none of your seeking and finding who lived *here*. Yes! He gave me your Diermit's talisman . . ." Dewi faltered as confusion slowed his remembering.

Madauc eyed him uncomfortably and attempted to pass the strange recitation off with raillery and reminiscence. "Mad Dewi! It seems old Diermit wasn't the only addled visionary. But not much wonder, in his case. Poor Diermit lived a thin, scrabbling life on the rocky edges of Lund. He would not come up into the castle or the green fields, and so we smuggled food for him in exchange for hearing over and over his visions and prophecies. Yet they were not all the shadows of his mind. When I was older, I lived for a time in Ireland, where my brother Rhirid holds a scrap of kingdom, and I heard the bards and storytellers there repeat much the same tales of Great Ireland and the legendary I Breasil, and of Saint Brendan's voyage to the Western Isles. Tales out of Dublin, where the Norsemen ruled, tell of the voyage of Thorfinn Karlsefni to a land called Vinland. Such tales are everywhere, but though wise men sense there must be truth at the heart of them, most still laugh and call them childish dreams. *They* are the fools! The islands *are* there. Vinland is there, and south of it the wide, rich islands of sunshine and apples where we shall glean our fortunes from the overflowing wealth of the seven cities of Antillia!"

In his excitement Madauc rose from the pallet on the stone floor to face the west door of the little church, and stretched his arms wide, as if he saw, through the walls and all the hills and the high curve of the sea between, to those western islands. He was so rapt in his imagined triumph that Dewi, too, began to picture marvelous landscapes painted on the walls themselves.

Neither heard Mailcun bark. But then the west door opened, shattering the imagined sea. The hermit stood bewildered by the expectant faces of the man and the boy. "You've not heard already? How could you?"

Madauc looked a little sheepish at being discovered in his enthusiasm. "Heard what?" he asked. He had not caught the note of deep concern in Gruffyt's voice.

"A lad who came for honey brought the news from Llanrwst market but an hour ago. Arthfael and Merfyn, the sons of Caradog, have come home to Trefriw, and they should know." The old man was agitated and found it difficult to say on.

"Arthfael and Merfyn? But they are my men! Men of the

teulu of Ywein. What is it they 'should know'? And why are they come here from the south instead of to Aberffraw?"

"Because Ywein Gwynet is dead."

Madauc sat down heavily, suddenly pale.

"Is it sure?" he asked at last.

"Aye. He lies in state in Bangor Cathedral. Within the month Prince Hywel will be acclaimed king at Aberffraw in Von."

Madauc, stunned, shook his head. Hywel and Iorwerth and many others had expected this, but Ywein's youngest son had shut the possibility from his mind. Ywein Gwynet dead, and the chance of recognition dead with him. Madauc spoke vaguely at first, as if explaining it all to himself. "Arthfael and Merfyn are in Trefriw? Why then, the *teulu* is scattered. My men are returning to their homes. Hywel has his own bodyguard and thinks he does not need our father's men." The old man and the boy saw him waver and then straighten himself with a new hardness as bleak as a winter day. "Well, the more fool he!" said Madauc, and his laughter had a note at once bitter and exultant to it. "There is our crew, Dewi lad! A hundred men, and two score of them the best sailors on the Irish Sea. Winter or no, we shall build *Gwennan Gorn* under Hywel's nose and sail with the coming of spring! And they will come, every one of them. What man will shy off when there's wealth and fame to be had? Come, dear good old Gruffyt!" He turned the full force of his disarming smile and his considerable will upon the old hermit. Only his eyes were cold. "How soon can you have Arthfael here from Trefriw?"

Gruffyt, the hermit, shrugged helplessly and sighed. "Soon," he said.

6

The Narrowing Ring

By early December Madauc, taking Dewi with him, had gone north through Rhos to the coast to find a haven for the building of *Gwennan Gorn*. After a few days, word was passed for the *teulu* to gather at the abandoned farm at Aber Kerrik, near the mouth of the river Ganol. Encroaching swamplands had long ago swallowed up its fields. The approach had become more a causeway than a road and could be easily defended.

Of the hundred, forty came, some out of loyalty to their *penteulu*, others simply for their love of the wild sea, and the rest because their pockets were empty and they had neither land nor families to tie their hearts to Gwynet. The forty laughed over their mead cups and said that the sixty who sent such regretful excuses had no stomach for the sea, and then manfully strove to drink each other under the table to prove who had the strongest stomach of all.

Trees were felled in the forest of Nant Gwynant for firewood and for ship's timbers; roofs were mended and walls patched to make the smaller of the tumbledown barns of Aber Kerrik snug quarters for the men; and the larger barn, being adjacent to the stone pier on the Afon Ganol not far from where that small river met the sea, was admirably suited for a boathouse. By the time the last great log had been dragged in and the firewood stacked so high that the barns looked like monstrous woodpiles, there was little to do but wait for the worst of winter to be gone. The laying of the keel of the ship was begun with the first and best-cured wood. Sleep, food, and drink, the stitching of heavy linen sails, the tanning of hides and the salting down of meat in earthen crocks, and the carving of nails, fair-leads, and bollards from staghorn (for iron nails too often snapped in the strain of a heavy sea)—these activities filled the days. Dewi found himself clerk of the company, drawing up lists of supplies and provisions for a long voyage: tar and wax; leather bottles for water and mead; honey, hard bread, and grain. More beef. More salt. An endless list.

The winter promised to be noisy, warm, and lazy; full of fights, bragging, and tall tales. The Companions of the Western Sea, as they now named themselves, kept much indoors, for Madauc did not wish to advertise how many they were and arouse the suspicion of the coastal guard who, happily for them, kept a conscientious watch only on that stretch of his shore nearest the tavern three miles distant, at Colwyn.

In the evenings Madauc drank as deeply as any of the Companions and laughed as loudly, but Dewi noticed that he never joined in the bragging contests or sang the bawdy or sad songs the others fancied. His tales were all of voyagers and treasure, wealth and the Western Isles; and he played on his men's desires as a harpist fingers his strings.

Winter's got in his heart, Dewi thought, and it made him a little uneasy. But he shrugged the thought away, telling himself he was sounding like old Gruffyt; sounding like his own old self. *His own old self?* He puzzled at the expression. When *had* he left off loving only the crisp lines of words and the sharply outlined paintings in books and joined his heart to this warm and unpredictable confusion? Had he truly meant to run away, to trade the world for the scratching of pens in a speechless monastery book room? He rolled over on his sheepskin blanket, making Mailcun a pillow for his head, and listened as Red Kynon, at Madauc's right hand, sang to the drowsing warriors the ancient lullaby of little Dinogad.

> *"Dinogad's speckled petticoat*
> *is made of skins of speckled stoat;*
> *whip whip whipalong,*
> *eight times we'll sing the song.*
> *When your father hunted the land,*
> *spear on shoulder, club in hand,*
> *thus his speedy dogs he'd teach,*
> *Giff, Gaff, catch her, catch her, fetch, fetch!*
> *In his coracle he'd slay*
> *fish as a lion does its prey.*
> *When your father went to the moor,*
> *he'd bring back heads of stag, fawn, boar,*
> *the speckled grouse's head from the mountain,*
> *fishes' heads from the falls of Oak Fountain.*
> *Whatever your father struck with his spear,*
> *wild pig, wild cat, fox from his lair,*
> *unless it had wings it would never get clear."*

"Giff, Gaff, dhaly dhaly dhwg dhwg," Red Kynon sang once more in the quiet hall.

"Had you not better sing, '*Me maris anfractus lustranda et littora terrent*'—'All those bending seas and shores to be crossed, they terrify me'?"

The sharp voice and the chill wind from the open door cut like knives. Men sat up blinking. Mailcun came awake with a snort.

Llywarch pushed the heavy door shut, stamped the new-fallen snow from his boots, and eyed the Companions with mock disbelief. "Lord! What a barnful of overgrown boys! The whole of Gwynet is under arms, and here you sit snug between swamp and shore, scarce three miles from

Castell Degannwy on the one side and Castell Colwyn on the other!"

"Nonsense." Madauc laughed, recovering from his surprise. "We've seen but one coast guard since we came, and there are none but old men and boys at Degannwy and Colwyn. Come, warm yourself by the fire, Prydyt y Moch. I confess, I'd almost given you up."

Dewi saw a flicker in the poet's eyes. "Those old men and boys will soon have company," he drawled. "The king thinks to move the royal court to Degannwy and leave Aberffraw to the crows and choughs. So, when old Gruffyt told me where you'd gone, I thought I'd best come snatch the lambs from the wolf's mouth."

Every man in the hall, drunk or sober, waked to alarm. Degannwy? Why should Hywel come to Degannwy? Queen Cristin lived there, and she hated Hywel as she hated all of the sons of Ywein except her own whelps Davyt and Rodri.

Madauc strode to the fire and pulled Llywarch roughly around to face him. "Have done with games! What is it? What's gone wrong? Hywel hasn't learned of your trick?"

"No." Llywarch's cat's eyes gleamed. "Nor has Davyt. Though, because you'd disappeared without a trace, Davyt had it I'd murdered you, a pleasure he hopes to reserve to himself. He kindly bade me hold an iron out of the fire while I swore I knew nothing of you dead or alive. I have left off harping for the winter, look you." He turned his hands palms up, and his lazy grin mocked Madauc's sharp intake of breath at the sight of the livid half-healed burns. Dewi came close to see and felt shamed at remembering his past distrust of the poet. It should have been enough that Madauc knew him for a true friend.

"Davyt?" Madauc frowned. "Why should Davyt be concerned?"

Llywarch shrugged maddeningly. "Why? Perhaps be-

cause Prince Davyt happens now to be King Davyt of Gwynet. You say you've not seen soldiers here in Rhos? That is your reason. Prince Davyt and Prince Rodri and the men of Rhos and Tegeigl crossed over to Von four days ago. King Hywel rose from the first feast of Christmas and came out from Aberffraw with his warband to oppose them. He met his death on a field near Pentraeth, and the seven sons of Cadifor died at his side. Eight red flowers spreading on the snowy field." Llywarch's voice trembled slightly, betraying the same horror that filled the others.

Madauc recovered himself in a moment. He spoke bitterly. "This has to be the doing of the witch Cristin, my father's widow. She has hated Hywel more than any, for he was first among those who stood between the kingdom and her own precious two."

"It is only the beginning," Llywarch said. "Next it will be Prince Kynon, and then Edwal and Maelgwn; perhaps even Rodri. Iorwerth may be safe. He at least treasures up no ambition. But what of you? You are caught in a cleft stick. You have no boat, and here you sit between Davyt's strongest castles. Indeed, I think I should have stayed away and sent a priest to shrive you all. I *should* be in Degannwy." He dropped into a mocking tone of complaint.

"Holy saints, *why?*"

"Um, ha. Well, it seems I am bard to Davyt now. Indeed, I have made him an ode and called it 'Ode to the Hot Iron,' which I mean to present to him on his arrival at Degannwy. He has sent me ahead to oversee the preparations for his coming. And to set spies out for news of you." His eyelids drooped. "I have sent them south into Rhufoniog and Nantconwy."

"You . . . you *madman!*" Madauc could not help laughing. The *teulu* crowded around, grinning and pressing brimming horns of mead upon Prydyt y Moch, who shrugged his cloak onto the floor and drained the largest of the horns offered to him before retiring with Madauc to a bench a little back from the fire. Dewi had an uneasy twinge as he heard Madauc, coldly thoughtful, say, "I give Davyt two years: one until our return, another for me to gather the men of Von and Arfon. And I will, with or without Maelgwn's leave. We can finish laying the keel of *Gwennan Gorn* tomorrow. We can be off before the winter turns into spring. It will be risky. Any of us who are known in Rhos must keep out of sight, and those who see to gathering provisions will have to be minding their tongues around taverns and wenches. Well. Do you come with us?"

"I'd as leave try it in a sea-going coracle. No, my lord, life on the ocean lacks too many of the comforts I have gotten attached to." Llywarch stretched his legs out to the fire. "Fires, for one thing. Good wine and roast lamb for another. Rich garments. Fighting the English. And lasses. There's one particular . . ."

"Ah well, then!" Madauc beckoned Dewi to bring another horn cup of mead. "You're done for, Prydyt y Moch. She'll muddle your wits, and then what will you live on in this deathly land?" He rose impatiently, finishing his mead in one long draft.

"Why should I fret?" Llywarch shrugged. "If I die tomorrow, today at least has been amusing."

Dewi shivered despite the fire and turned back to his bed. There, with the talisman a heavy, insistent weight between his hand and breast, he wondered at his father's friends. Llywarch thought to wrap himself safe from past and future in the pleasure of the moment, but it was the past that held Madauc fast. Today, tomorrow: they were only means to yesterday, to restoring lost love, honor withheld, hurt pride, and the birthright owing to the son of Ywein. *Man folds his wings,* said Diermit's riddling prophecy. Llywarch and Madauc, poet and prince: did each tread his own narrowing ring? Warmth and cheer had faded from the hall in the chill wind that swept Llywarch through their door. Winter ruled Gwynet with violence, as it had that long-ago place from where Diermit's riddle had come, somewhere beyond the western sea. Dewi drifted over the edge of sleep wondering how wise it was to leave Gwynet and its familiar evils for . . . for what? A shadow in the west? *Spreading white sails. White wings. Perhaps it would all come right. Everything would come right when they found Antillia. The Fortunate Isles.* His old dream of the great river and the strange city was only a shadow behind new images, brilliant and confused. There would be fountains of youth, and the apple trees were silver, the apples pearls . . .

II
CIBOTLÁN

1
Landfall

She was a beautiful ship, a straight-keeled, single-masted *nailong,* to give her the name the Irish gave the ships of the Norsemen. Dewi pulled with the men on the ropes to bring her up onto the sandy beach at the head of the great bay, and wondered how he could have thought her squat and awkward on that cold February day, three months gone, when she went down the wooden slide into the river Ganol. Dewi had learned much about the sea and knew now that those things that made her homely were themselves her beauty. Fifty feet long, and broader in the beam than Norse vessels, *Gwennan Gorn* was perhaps a little tubby, but she was more buoyant because of it. Madauc had used every seaman's trick he knew to make her unsinkable. Her timbers were well joined, the oak planking tightly overlapped, her joints well tarred; and to make her further proof against the water and swifter in it, she was covered with tanned hides well stretched and stitched and then smeared with wax. She steered a little sluggishly, perhaps, so that only Madauc and one or two others could steer an arrow-straight wake with her heavy stern rudder in a good breeze; but she stood up under heavy winter seas, riding into the wind with the sweep of twenty oars, her square white sail furled. At night her tilt—a canopy stretched over a line from the high bowsprit to mast to sternpost—kept the worst of the weather from the men, who slept and watched in turns.

Their course had been southward from the end of land

that was westernmost Britain to the northwesternmost point of Spain. It was a course several had sailed before, among them Red Kynon, Madauc's second-in-command, a sailor long before he had turned soldier. They and all of the seamen had hard work of it, for the landsmen among the forty were continually ill and worse than useless in the mountainous sea. The hound Mailcun was miserable and troublesome and in the worst weather had to be lashed into a makeshift harness by the mast so that he would not be swept overboard.

Farther south the weather improved, and happily no French or Portugee Arab ships came out to harass them. At an isolated seacoast farm where they put in for water and were able to buy fruit and vegetables, the farm laborers shook their heads mournfully over the madness of foreigners.

Off Lisboa the Companions flew into the sunshine with the best of northwesterly winds bellying out the square white sail. And as the land bent eastward toward the Pillars of Hercules, they kept a southwesterly course into the open sea. It was at sunset on the eleventh day out from land that they sighted the islands legend and Diermit, the seer, had named the Islands of the Moon, rising rose and gold out of the darkening sea. These islands lay, so the tales of seamen had it, one day west of the land of the Ethiops. For the Companions they were the edge of the world, and every man breathed more easily knowing that they, at least, were more than legend. On the largest island a few farmers tilled the rich land and tended vineyards. One, an elderly Arab, had enough Latin to haggle with Dewi and Red Kynon over the price of sea salt and rabbits and six sheepskins of the island's wine. Oleanders and goats' cheese scented the air, and even cactus, desert hills, and the brooding snow mountain of El Teide seemed sweet and good when the men thought of the wide ocean;

and sweeter yet when they had left them weeks behind.

Beset by spring squalls and running under sail, *Gwennan Gorn* struggled all the fifth week out from the islands to beat westward aslant the black storm at her back that rolled so relentlessly northward. "Magic," the men called *Gwennan Gorn*. It seemed nothing could sink her. But in their gaunt faces and shadowed eyes sat a deeper, haunting fear: that they would beat on endlessly into mist and darkness, dead men on a soaring ship. When at the beginning of the sixth week from land they were blown among islands, they wept for joy. Uncanny green jewels of islands in a black sea under a leaden sky. Islands where strange trees, tall and slender, whipped their fronds in the storm like green girls swinging their hair in the wind.

But they could not land for the storm and were swept westward in an arc into a calmer sea, to stand to at last off a small flat island with a few storm-tattered trees and a fresh-water spring. Not I Breasil, not even Tir na'nOg, the elvish land of summer, could have been more welcome. Every man except Madauc and the two he kept with him swam ashore to caper unsteadily and roar their delight, hugging the rocks and embracing every ragged tree. Madauc watched, but he scarcely saw. The conviction that the lovely islands of the storm were those Isles of Llion sought long ago by the Briton Gafran ap Aeddan, and that Antillia and its riches must be close at hand, obsessed him. From the signs of wind and water and the flight of sea birds, he determined that some mass of land lay not far away, but more to the north than west. The waterskins refilled, he drove the Companions on when they would have rested.

And so they came to land, through the mouth of a wide bay. Her mast unstepped, *Gwennan Gorn* was beached and dragged across log rollers, set under her keel, over the sand and tussocks of wiry grass to a hiding place under the eaves of the forest that crowded against the dunes as if to swallow them and march against the water itself. The Companions wove screens of branches and left her there.

At the head of the bay two broad rivers, and between them smaller streams, flowed down from the north. The country around was an intricate maze of creeks, marshes, and islands overgrown with a tangle of mangrove trees, and farther inland, the nearer—the westernmost—of the rivers was strewn with the trunks of great trees rotting along the marshy banks where they had fallen. The men wore the boots they had brought for the cold weather of the northern seas, for they kept out more than water—leeches and biting insects—and could afford some protection against the poisonous-looking vipers they saw swimming in the sluggish water of the swampy areas.

It was along the nearer, the broad western waterway, that Madauc and the Companions marched, armed and carrying on their backs the meager provisions left to them, tied up in their cloaks. But they found neither men nor villages nor roads and began to fear they had come to some great desert land and not Antillia. One or two began to mutter that it would take a mountain of gold to make up for such discomfort and such short rations.

The forest was deep, tangled, and forbidding. Madauc was reluctant to explore beyond its fringes, for even a short twenty yards from the riverbank brought them into a dark gray-green world untouched by the sun, draped with creeping vines and long beards of moss, or woven with great thickets of flowering greenthorn that climbed thirty feet and more to twine in the branches of young trees and smother them. Shaggy black willow, oak trees, chestnuts, hornbeams: even these trees they thought they recognized were larger, heavier, strangely unfamiliar. Once, the line of men crossed a narrow track worn smooth and deep; but if by its straightness it suggested a track made by men, in its narrowness it seemed an unlikely one. Yet what deer would travel so? At last, aching with the unaccustomed exertion of the march, the men persuaded their captain to make camp in a small clearing near the watersmeet where a tributary from the north poured into the great river at the point where it came flowing out of the east.

Dewi was glad of the strangeness. While the Companions gathered firewood and boughs and rushes for making beds —to the accompaniment of great groans at their stiffness and soreness and voluble complaints about the emptiness of their bellies—Dewi moved slowly, caught up in the wonder of the dank jungle-wood where black squirrels whisked up into a green dimness and giant spider webs gleamed like dull silver traceries on the face of the dark. Insects swarmed: midges. He slapped at his neck and arms continually, and the ground was soggy underfoot.

This must be Alabama, or Mississippi. The thought flapped dustily in his mind, aimlessly, to be brushed away as easily as a moth. The names seemed familiar, and yet they meant nothing to him. Nor did Antillia. It was not at all what he had expected. No apple gardens. None of the jeweled fountains of Madauc's tales. Nor was it like the dream. When had it first come to him, that dream of a wide river running among the knees of wooded hills? It seemed always to have been with him. Beyond the hills there had been fields of grass and grain. Cattle. And strange gray cities, roads like ribbons of stone. But if this were the place—and he could not remember why he had thought his dreamland lay here beyond the western sea—it was not as he had dreamed it, and he was glad. Memory of that past-future had slipped from his grasp, but to him it seemed no loss, only a weight of nightmare fallen away. A dream of the future: yes, that was what it had been. As vivid as this strange real world he walked in, true vision or not, it had no meaning for him; was no concern of his. It had come back to him at sea sometimes in the hour before waking, to frighten him. The men had laughed and said he cried out not in Welsh, but in a strange gibberish a little like the bits of English they knew. "Is that the tongue they speak in Antillia, mad Dewi?" They would tease him until an irritated Madauc ordered them to leave the boy in peace.

Dewi was thankful to be left alone, but he suspected that Prince Madauc's ill temper had its source in the suspicion that the taunt was aimed as much at Antillia as at mad Dewi. Madauc's fear was that his dream of Antillia might be illusion, might hold no more of sense than Dewi's gibberish. He did not laugh any more. Thin now, gaunt-eyed and restless, he had drawn apart and into himself from the night Llywarch brought the news of Hywel's death and laughed at their boyhood oath and would not come. From the slowness of his movements at waking, and other things, Dewi guessed that Madauc's old wound sometimes pained him. Winter, work, and the harsh sea had worn away more than laughter.

Dewi returned to the clearing with an armful of boughs to find a fire roaring and many of the company sprawled half asleep on heaps of leafy boughs. Five or six, seated in a circle, were already deep in a fierce game of chance improvised with pebbles and lines scratched in the earth, wagering their shares in the gold that was to come. Close by, Merfyn skinned out a young doe he had shot, while his brother Arthfael, a short, dark young man, rigged a roasting spit across the fire. Red Kynon had sharpened his knife to a razor edge and set up as barber, beginning with Madauc himself. When the carcass had been spitted, Madauc ordered Dewi to keep it turning and the fire fed.

"The lad's as weary as any of us, Captain," Red Kynon said mildly as Madauc rose, rubbing his chin. "I'll take it over after I've seen to my bed and my gear. I'll need to be tireder yet before I can sleep without a deck rolling under me."

"As you wish." The words were cold, uninterested. Madauc turned abruptly on his heel and strode up the riverbank to disappear in the thin mist that gathered in the early dusk. Red Kynon shook his head, but Dewi understood—though he was not sure how he came to do so. It was the sick feeling of doubt, the nightmare that you had taken a wrong turning into a strange, unfriendly world from which there was no turning back. He felt a momentary impulse to run after Madauc, to say, "We will find the seven cities. I know we will. And I will mind the fire." But he held back. He was no puppy to go fawning after a master; at least not when he would get only a sharp word for his pains.

Hours later, when the men slept with bellies full of good roast venison, their captain still had not returned. Alarmed, Red Kynon had posted a larger night guard than was customary with the *teulu*, but would allow none of the men to search more than a few yards up and downstream. "A fool's trick, looking for a man by moonlight in a mist like this. Keep your ears pricked, and mind you stay in sight. If there *is* anyone else out there, they'll be liking nothing better than picking us off one by one."

That men might be stalking them, keeping abreast deep in the forest, had not occurred to Dewi. Surely they would have seen some trace of men along the river? But not, he realized with a shiver, if the river itself were the only road. They might easily slip ashore in the mist and could have come upon Madauc unawares. Red Kynon was probably right to hold back from searching; but he had forgotten Mailcun.

Using the excuse that he wished to soften a lump of pitch to mend an empty water bottle, Dewi took a brand from the fire to his place at the circle's outer edge. No one saw him light the tallow dip in the lantern he had carried with his share of the stores. He closed the shutter on the light and hid it under a bush, in easy reach. Ten minutes later, with a touch to rouse and warn the dog, he rolled from his rustling bed and lay still, his hand on the lantern's iron ring handle. Red Kynon did not turn. The clearing's edge was only a few yards away. A guard passed. Swiftly, keeping low to the ground, Dewi ran for the cover of the trees, Mailcun's nose at his heels.

The darkness was chill, frightening: a damp blindfold that made it seem there was, there could be, no world but what he held in his own heart. It was as if he had passed, quite literally, into the dark of the moon. Panicky, he drew his breath in gulps, as if even the air might disappear. "Up" and "down" eluded him; they were words without meaning.

It's the dream, he thought in sudden panic. There was the same awful darkness between now and that other place. With a great effort he recalled himself, choking back the impulse to call out for help.

But he did not dare uncover the lantern here. Red Kynon would see it. Then Mailcun whimpered and pushed against him, and, turning, Dewi saw the glimmer of the campfire. The river . . . there was no safety away from the river or the fire. "The water," he whispered in command; and he followed the hound in a wide arc around fire and clearing to the river's edge. Upstream, a night bird called, the call muffled in the mist to a plaintive, almost human cry. Every light splash on the unseen water Dewi imagined a muffled oar-stroke from a boat of Antillian soldiers. The lantern was worse than useless. It made the fog a solid, glaring barrier, and so he shut it down again. The moonlight turned the mist to shreds of silvery gauze and, closer to the ground, a thick whiteness that chilled his ankles and tried to betray him into the river. Twice he walked into large trees growing on the bank. Mailcun padded ahead, nose to the ground, disappearing and then coming back to see that he had not lost his master.

The dog had been gone for some minutes when Dewi, cast adrift, became dimly aware of a presence in the fog, keeping pace with him, frightened, more lost than he. Close by, no more than a few yards to his left, the whiteness swirled and eddied around some movement other than his own, and he thought he heard a voice whispering to itself: a sound like the nervous rustling of leaves. But there was no breeze. Curiously, Dewi was not alarmed. It seemed almost an appointed meeting . . . a meeting, or escape, or refuge from. . . .He moved nearer, until a slight thinning of the mist showed him a stumbling figure, itself half mist; the Dewi from his half-forgotten dream—*Dave now*—groping with his eyes shut like a sleepwalker's, against the blinding fog. Dewi watched him eagerly. Had the dream after all been of now and not the far future? Then the great castled cities and highways that gleamed in the sun like ribbons of satin might after all exist, perhaps on the upper reaches of this same river . . . *now*. And the Companions might have a chance at the riches they hungered for after all.

Caution made Dewi hold his tongue. How odd and alien the boy looked! The close-cropped hair, the dreaming face, the oddly striped clothing (the word *pajamas* flickered and faded in his memory) clinging, damp with the fog. Dewi followed, fascinated, Madauc and Mailcun forgotten.

The boy's rustling whisper grew more unsure with each step. *Where am I? Where is this? Someone called. But no one's here, and I can't find the way. . . . Please . . .*"

"Look out!" Dewi called out sharply. "You'll dream yourself into the river, the way you're going. Wake up!"

The other stopped, swaying, his eyes open but unfocused.

"*Who is that?*" he whispered, peering around, fixing at last on Dewi's solid figure in the drifting whiteness. "*Why won't you let me alone? What do you want from me? I don't know you . . .*" The words faded as the boy backed nervously away from the recognition that stirred between them. The fog-shrouded riverbank hung outside of time as the two boys stared at each other, each mistrustful, wary. Hesitantly, Dewi pulled the silver talisman out, frowning at it in puzzlement.

"*No! You keep it!*" the other boy cried. "*I won't take it back. I won't go back.*" His pajama-clad figure, as thin and unsubstantial as the fog, flickered and was gone.

Dazed, Dewi slowly thrust the silver roundel inside the neck of his tunic. The boy was real then and not a dream; but not . . . not here-and-now either. The where and when of him was too much to unmuddle, too hard for explaining. "Mad Dewi," he thought wryly, and shivered despite himself. Mad Dewi had best hold his tongue about the boy—and the great cities. Let the cities of Antillia discover themselves. He must find Madauc. He angled cautiously toward the riverbank and whistled softly.

But a crashing in the underbrush had already sent the hound back in scrambling haste. Mailcun had scented deer in the distance, but the damp air had deceived him, and he had walked between the legs of a large buck drinking at the river's edge. Both boy and dog, considerably shaken, went more carefully and watched more than the ground at their feet. It was Mailcun who saw Madauc first. The hound had moved away from the river and came back to bring Dewi along. He stood pointing, and the boy stopped beside him to stare across the small clearing where the forest drew back a little from the river and a light breeze swept the mist away.

Madauc lay fast asleep where weariness had overtaken him, stretched on the moonlit grass beside a small stream flowing out from the wood. It seemed a pity to have to wake him back to worry. The harshness that had grown upon him was softened, and his face seemed young again. Dewi hesitated, undecided what to do; but then the dog growled softly, backing against his knees in warning. A bird called: two falling notes.

"What is it, lad?" Dewi knelt as he whispered. He touched Mailcun lightly, then drew his hand away. The hackles were raised in a wide, stiff ridge down the hound's back, and he stood rigid, a growl vibrating in his throat. Dewi looked where the dog stared. Startled, he reached down to make a sign for quiet.

A still figure stood at the wood's edge, moonlit against its blackness. Slowly the figure moved forward, as if drawn through the bright grass toward the sleeping man: drawn and yet reluctant. It was a girl; or woman. She was slender, bare-legged, her long hair hanging like a dark waterfall below the waist of a short robe. Like a sleepwalker she moved to stand, hands to her cheeks, at the young man's feet. Instinctively, Dewi knew that this was no apparition drawn across time or out of a dream, but flesh and blood, and dangerous. He knew he should call out to warn Madauc, yet something in her agitation held back his words. He wished he could see her face. Spellbound, he watched her move closer, kneel, and slowly reach out in wonder to touch the bright hair that fell back from Madauc's brow. His hair gleamed and seemed to spill the moonlight into the waves of silver grass. She bent, her dark hair like a cloud across the moon. A scene out of some ancient elvish tale . . .

Then Mailcun barked and broke the spell.

The girl sprang up, and Dewi ran. He leaped the little stream, calling, "Wait! Come back!" but she ran like a deer. Madauc sat up dazedly and pushed himself erect to

stand, blinking, swaying, thinking himself still in a dream. He watched, bewildered, as the hound Mailcun gained on the fleeing girl and streaked behind and beyond her, throwing his weight at the back of her knees as he passed, to break her stride and balance. She went sprawling, and Dewi came up as she was scrambling to her hands and knees.

"Here! Wait, will you? We don't mean to hurt you," he panted. He reached for her arm, but she swung away. He had caught hold of the thick, dark hair and was yelling over and over, "I won't hurt you," when she swung back around with a doublehanded blow that caught him below the breastbone and drove the breath from him. He fell, blind and astonished, with Madauc's laughter ringing after him into the darkness.

"Come, on your feet, then! Next time you must try for an ankle. Or wait until you're grown a man!" Madauc was still laughing as he hauled Dewi to his feet and gave him a brutal openhanded blow on the back to help him breathe again. It brought tears, too, but it worked. "Who on earth was she? What happened, lad?"

Dewi gasped and drew a shuddering breath. "I don't know. Is she g-gone?"

Madauc drew him from the moonlight under the shadowed edge of the wood. "Yes. But Mailcun's gone, too. Listen!" The dog's belling call rang dimly through the trees. "Was she alone?"

"I think so." Dewi described what he had seen.

Madauc frowned. "I don't like it. It makes no sense. One slip of a girl in an empty land?"

Mailcun sounded nearer, giving tongue as if he ran again with Iorwerth's pack, harrying a doe upon the hills of Nantconwy.

Madauc listened. "She's circling around, heading upstream a way. Well, are you all right?" When Dewi nodded, he said, "Come, then. Fetch that lantern you say you brought. We'll make our way along the wood's edge until she comes between us and the dog."

They had not gone far when they were brought up short by the cry of that same night bird Dewi had heard earlier: a high, despairing cry. But this time it was answered by a single piping note, a note that rang out and died and rang again. It came from a little way ahead, among the trees.

"A signal. And she is homing on it," Madauc said grimly. He unsheathed the long dagger that hung at his belt. "I would to heaven I'd my sword by me. Once a fool, ever a fool, it seems. And no Llywarch to save us this time with one of his sleight-of-hand tricks." He went ahead cautiously.

The dog's baying stopped; and then in a moment, close by, he set up an angry, baffled barking, as if he had cornered something that he feared. There were no voices of men, no cries, only the frantic barking and a light, high scream of breath like the hissing of a great snake.

Madauc reached for the lantern Dewi carried and pulled the shutter free. The darkness almost swallowed up its narrow, guttering beam. As he swung it across the crowding tree trunks, they saw Mailcun and then the girl.

She stood trembling, pale as death, her back against a tree, her great dark eyes defying them. The long hair was pushed back, tangled in the cord of a heavy sack slung hurriedly across her shoulders, and they saw for the first time the flower tattooed on one cheek and the strange signs pricked down one leg. In her arms she held a little boy, and tethered to the tree where the child had slept in a nest among the roots, a great spotted cat screamed and strained against its golden chain.

2
Coala

Madauc smeared the long, raking claw marks on Mailcun's face and neck with a healing salve from the Companions' small and precious store of medicines while Dewi watched and made encouraging noises. The great cat was dead, brought down by a well-thrown knife, and each of the men had a link of the golden chain for trophy, but it was brave Mailcun who bore the battle scars. The dog sat obediently, eyes closed and his lip trembling over his teeth in a grimace equally expressive of pain and humiliation. The doctoring finished, Dewi stood, and it was then that he noticed the girl.

For hours she had sat at the edge of the camp circle, still and proud, clutching the little boy and her sack of belongings. The child had slipped free at last and now sat contentedly on Red Kynon's knee. Dewi, speechless, gave a sharp nudge to Red Kynon, who looked up to stare, awestruck, over the dark head of the little boy. The child placidly went on chewing at a juicy bit of venison rib.

"Holy heaven bless us!" Red Kynon said. "Will you not have a look at that, Captain? I think it wants a word with you!"

Madauc thrust the pot of salve into the large wallet bag that hung at his side and followed his lieutenant's glance.

The girl approached nervously, ceremoniously. A light cloak, blue and richly embroidered with white and blue feathers, floated out behind her. A heavy collar made of curious gold links hung more than halfway to her waist;

gold snakes twined around her wrists and ankles; and a strange emblem of green stones rose from a gold circlet on her brow. The shabby sack had held treasure fit for a queen.

Merfyn whooped and pointed. The Companions set up a rowdy, excited clamor, crowding close around, touching and exclaiming until Madauc—as excited at the sight of so much gold as the others—thought to warn them back. The girl kept on, trembling a little, until to Madauc's great astonishment she fell to her knees at his feet, slipping her hands around his ankles and touching her forehead to his mud-caked boots.

"*Coala kwutlá'uwá 'untutl-kwutluí, 'untutlukallín!*" She peered up at him with a tentatively hopeful smile.

"Good lord, what is the girl about? What in the name of all the saints can she want?" Madauc stared down at her in alarm, then looked from Red Kynon to Dewi with a scowl of perplexity that brought laughter from his men. "What the devil do you suppose she's saying?"

The girl trembled at his frown. "*Coala kwutlá'uwá . . . 'untutlukallín?*" She proceeded to lay her forehead once more on his boots.

"Kynon," Madauc grated, hard put to keep from laughter despite his impatience, "stop laughing like the great idiot you are and pry her loose of my feet. We must find where she comes from. If all the maids there wear such gold as this, our fortunes are made!"

Red Kynon put the little boy down from his knee and leaned over to pull the girl gently by the elbow. She did not move. Dewi, still very much aware of the painful bruise where her blow had driven the silver talisman against his chest, was a little less gentle as he in turn tried to loosen her grip. He felt the quiver in her taut muscles and let go at last, looking sheepish.

"I think she's frightened," he said.

"She has no reason to be." Madauc waved his hand impatiently. "She cannot think we make war on women and children. Perhaps it is her trinkets she fears for." He looked down at the small heart-shaped face that was lifted to peer at him. It was a strangely disturbing face: high, broad cheekbones and a fine, high-bridged nose. This alien delicacy was deepened by the dark, woeful eyes and the blue flower tattooed on her right cheek. She was not a child, he saw, nor yet a woman. He did not like it. If the maids of this land were all so, he would have hard work to keep his men's minds on gold, let alone on Gwynet. More, there was something in the way the girl looked at him that was disquieting, almost frightening: like the ewe with a broken leg who offers her throat to the wolf-dog who finds her cowering in a hollow among the rocks; like the bird held by the snake's eye.

"Keep your hands to yourself," he snapped at two of the men who had squatted down beside the girl to fondle the heavy linked collar and feel its weight. Reaching down to raise her up himself, he found to his surprise that she stood willingly. "Well!" He smiled briefly, the moment's misgivings gone. "She'll not be dealing with the rest of you, it seems. Come, scholar Dewi! How are we to find what we wish to know? You might try her with your Latin or your gibberish English. Ask her about the gold."

The girl listened earnestly, but kept her eyes on the prince. After each question she shook her head helplessly. Dewi, in desperation, pointed to his captain and, speaking loudly, as if she were a hard-of-hearing and not very intelligent dog, repeated, "Prince Madauc. *Ma*-dauc!"

"M-Matec?" She pronounced it hesitantly, in a puzzled tone. "*Ma*tec? E! Matec. *Ioquí Coala.*" She pointed to herself and then to the little boy. "Coala. Tochtlú."

"Coala?" Madauc waved Dewi aside and began trying to make himself understood through signs, all the time watching the girl with a cold intensity of excitement that made Dewi bite his lip. He looked at her as if he saw no more than gold and bright green stones, Dewi thought. It was a look that unnerved him. From the night of their flight from Dolwydlan, Dewi had drifted into a day-to-day life that revolved around one thing: Madauc and his dream. His own confused visions, his father's share in Madauc's dream—these had been too vague, too distant, and were swept up by the vision of wealth and power. But he was uneasy. In those first days Madauc had been as warm and easy with him as if he were a younger brother, but now he was grown abrupt and distant. More and more as the months passed, Dewi had felt that when Madauc looked at him, he stared through him, seeing only what purpose he could be put to; and now again Madauc's look aroused that slipping, unreasonable fear that he might be transparent in some true sense. If he could not sort memory from remembered dream; if Ithil sometimes wavered in the mind's eye and became a strangely familiar man in heavy outlandish clothing; if there was no seeing ahead to tomorrow—why, a look like that was like a blow. It canceled you. It whispered that you were not real.

But the girl Coala did not seem at all to mind. She watched and listened eagerly with her hands crossed upon her breast as Madauc made a sweeping gesture that included river, forest, all the land that spread away north and around them. "This country," he said, "it is Antillia, isn't it? An*till*ia? An-till-i-a?" He held up seven fingers. "Seven cities? Antillia?"

"Ante-illya?" She shook her head. Repeating Madauc's gesture, she said, *"Cibotlán. Iboquí Cibotlán."* When Madauc and the Companions showed no recognition of the name and the prince showed his disappointment with a muttered curse, she seemed to feel great distress. Hurriedly—yet Dewi sensed that it was reluctantly, too—

she held up seven fingers and nodded violently. Reaching out her arm, the gold snakes winking in the sun, she pointed to the west and announced, "*Natilchizcó!*" Indicating the north, she said, "*Tushcloshán,*" and to points farther east and north she gave the names "*Etowán, Cutivachcó, Ranoacán, Quaunatilcó, Tucrikán.*" Repeating these carefully as she counted them off on her fingers, she regarded Madauc anxiously, as if she wanted only to please. Yet it seemed to Dewi that when she saw how well she had succeeded in pleasing, she appeared more desperately anxious than before.

"*Seven cities!*"

The outburst that met the news rang in the woods and rolled away on the water. Madauc raised his arms, loosing in his joy and relief the terrible battle cry of Gwynet, and drank in the Companions' answering cry as if the day, the moment, were a draft of strong wine after a long thirst. "Cibotlán, is it?" He drew a deep breath. "The name is not the same, but that is nothing. Time and distance change more than names. What was it she named the city north along this river?"

"*Tush*-something?" Dewi said when none of the others could remember.

"*Tush*-something? Why so sulky, Dewi, lad? It's our fortunes we will be gathering there! It's what we've come for: a richer plunder than ever we took from Arwystli or Caer Vyrdin! *Tush*-what?" He turned questioningly to Coala.

"Tushcloshán," she prompted in a very small voice, a whisper hollow as a reed. Her hands scratched at each other.

"Tushcloshán. And is there gold in Tushcloshán? Gold? Here, this: *gold,*" Madauc insisted, pointing to her bracelets and jingling the links of the collar, then pointing off to the north. "Gold?"

"Come, Captain, you're frighting the poor thing," Red

Kynon murmured, but he got no more than a brief, impatient glance for it.

Dewi, unhappy, unsure why he felt so dismayed, turned away. Finding the solemn little boy playing patiently with a stick of wood, he sat and took him on his lap. What, he asked himself, had he thought they had come for, if not this? For what, if not raids, and death, and plunder? How else were they to return to Gwynet laden with riches? He had never asked himself in all these months. Were cities to open their gates and heap treasure upon the strange travelers from over the sea's edge? *I am a fool. I did not think. Must everything be as old Gruffyt saw in his vision? "Every tree, every stone and flower bled . . . and it was our own hearts we devoured so hungrily."*

Little Tochtlú leaned his head against Dewi's shoulder and, seeing a string, tugged at it. Diermit's talisman pulled free, and he played with it for a while very quietly. When he did look up, Coala was nodding tearfully and pointing northward, towards Tushcloshán, as she repeated Madauc's word, "Golt. *Iyeteúh* golt," with a sigh. A faintly puzzled, uneasy frown drew her dark brows together, as if she could not see why he should care so much about this "golt."

"Co'la?" lisped Tochtlú. "Co'la? *Kwutlú! 'Ntutl-kwutlú?*" He held up the talisman to show her his discovery.

Coala took one glance, scarcely a proper look, and with a cry she was once more on her knees at Madauc's feet. Dewi caught a gleam in her eye that set him to wondering if she were truly frightened. Or was she playing for time to think, to puzzle something out?

In a moment Madauc had pulled her back to her feet, saying—more gently than he had spoken before—"What is it? No one is going to hurt you. No one will take your pretty gold trinkets."

Apparently encouraged by his tone and knowing words

were useless, she pointed to Dewi and reached out her hand commandingly. At Madauc's nod he pulled the cord over his head and held out the talisman. She snatched it, to turn it over and over in dawning wonder. With great excitement she pointed from the small winged figure to Madauc himself. " *'Untutl-kwutlú! Iboquí 'untutlvocí patl. A Coala ikán teukallán 'untutlvocí!*" she cried, forgetting that they could not understand. Then, remembering, she pointed excitedly from the pendant to the north, and then to the gold emblem that was repeated in the links of her collar, and fell into an anxious silence.

The sign on each link was a bird, strangely feathered, scarcely recognizable as a bird, and nothing like a winged man. But each was circled, held within the ring of a snake that swallowed its own tail.

Dewi watched Madauc as he examined the emblems side by side. None of the men, not even Red Kynon, knew about the talisman or Diermit or the ancient prophecy; but seeing their captain's startled look of wonder, they all fell silent and drew back a little. Madauc himself showed a mixture of alarm and fascination, which they could not understand, and their bewilderment increased as he looked at the boy Dewi and softly spoke words almost as strange as the girl's.

> "*Man folds his wings*
> *To tread the narrowing ring;*
> *The serpent throned devours the circle*
> *and himself . . .*"

"What can it mean?" Madauc whispered. "Can it be the old man didn't lie? Can there *be* such things as oracles? Or an island of apple trees?"

The men wondered. Had their captain somehow understood the girl's chirping gabble? The girl Coala seemed equally unsure. Pointing once more to the north, she said hopefully, "*Di Abáloc. Abáloc?* 'Golt' *di* Abáloc. Golt?"

"*Avallach?*" Madauc stared.

The Companions exchanged unbelieving looks. Had they heard aright? *Avallach?* Avallach, the Avalon, the apple island of the old legends? No, it could not be. Their uneasiness deepened. Mortal men *could* not find Avallach. It was a magic place; forbidden. They muttered. There was too much here that was strange. Better to push ahead to the nearest castle, take what plunder they could, and win back to *Gwennan Gorn* before some wary coast guard found her.

But the word *Abáloc* had in its way as much power as the word "golt," which Coala had used so hopefully. Through signs and gestures Madauc determined that though the wide land of Cibotlán stretched perhaps ten days' journey northward, somewhere beyond lay the kingdom called Abáloc, which could be reached by boat upon a great river: a great river that ran between hills. Coala made signs with her hands: a delicate, rippling sweep of river; rounded, crowding hills.

Madauc's eyes met Dewi's, questioning. Something new moved in him, and seeing Dewi's answering excitement, he forgot for the moment what he had so long deemed his reason for their coming, and forgot the difficulties they faced in an inhospitable land.

"Abáloc, then!" he said, and a slow smile lit his face.

He did not, in his abstraction, see his men's dismay. But Coala took it all in. "Golt," she put in quickly. The men brightened a little at that, but still grumbled as they took up wallets and weapons and folded their cloaks, tying them in long rolls that went over the shoulder.

Madauc returned the talisman to Dewi and busied himself with his own gear. Dewi's head whirled. Was everything changed, then? He had seen a faint flush rise on Madauc's wind-browned cheeks when the girl's promise of gold in Abáloc had come so promptly. The girl was sharp. And she was right about the talisman. Dewi wondered how it was that he had not seen it before. The silver was worn quite smooth, but one portion of the ring was uneven, and he could just make out the shape of the head swallowing the tail—even one small eye—and around it what might have once been tiny scales graven on the metal. He felt elation, the excitement of fear and curiosity, and a deep stirring of relief he could not explain.

Abáloc!

3

The Deserted Lands

They traveled north along the river, keeping a sharp watch, relieved that they encountered no soldiers, and yet puzzled that their coming should go unnoted. On the fourth day, in higher country, the Companions sighted a small village ahead on the river's bank. Mystified and a little mistrustful, they watched the girl Coala don her golden regalia and walk alone to demand entrance at the gates. What words were spoken they could not hear; not that they could have understood, but they had an uneasy wait of it, not knowing. When in answer to a sign from the girl, Madauc led them after her, the village proved to be empty. Even the gatekeeper had fled. Yet it was no ambush. The villagers, it seemed, had run away into the woods on the far side of their huddle of mud and wattle houses. Coala wore an unhappy frown and slid sidelong glances at Prince Madauc, but he only ordered the men to look for food and to go warily. There was no gold. They found little in the tiny huts but dried beans and maize and another strange grain, and small hard cakes apparently made from ground chestnuts—all of which could be easily carried—and had soon supplied themselves and moved on. Some grew sullen and muttered against the girl, saying that she had warned the villagers to flee, taking their valuables with them. But others took turns at carrying little Tochtlú on their backs. The strung-out column averaged forty miles that day and on the days following. Merfyn, his feet badly blistered, swore that he would kiss the first horse he saw when they came home to Gwynet.

There were few natives to be seen in all these miles, though from time to time wide fields of green and growing crops climbed away from the river. Nevertheless, the news of their coming spread. One afternoon they were startled by an eerie music that struck up ahead, and they slowed uncertainly. Coming toward them was a band of villagers playing on reed pipes and jingling strings of small copper and silver bells, and escorting a dignified old man who rode on a litter borne by four smiling, buxom women.

"Now, there's a use for wives!" Red Kynon grinned. The others were more interested in the pearls embroidering the old man's short cloak and the gold pin that fastened it. "Every one as fine a pearl as my old father fishes out of Conwy, and many finer," one said.

From the gestures the old chief made in his speech to Coala, the Companions gathered that he invited them to his village. He bobbed his head up and down, and when Madauc made a sign of greeting, he bowed so vehemently that he was in danger of falling off his litter. " *'Untutlukallín Bopillá! 'Untutlukallín Bopillá,*" he cried.

The village of Bopillá consisted of some fifty neat log houses chinked with mud and thatched with straw, surrounded by a palisaded earthwork and standing in the middle of wide fields. The entire population had gathered beyond the gateway, and the path through the village was lined with offerings: little baskets of dried beans and maize, fish and dried meat, deerskins, lion and bear and cat skins. The skins should have been especially welcome, for clothing and boots were fast falling to pieces and much in need of patching or replacement; but the Companions passed everything by and peered into windows and doorways with ill-concealed impatience.

"No gold?" Red Kynon's ironic murmur went unheard.

Except by Coala. Stepping forward once more, she raised a commanding hand and spoke sharply to the old chief. A bewildered question, a sharp rebuke, perplexity, and nods and smiles followed in quick succession. In a moment the old man was fumbling at his cloak and his wives at their ears. Then with every appearance of delight, and to the embarrassed surprise of the men of Gwynet, the Chief Wife padded forward to place a gold cloak-pin and eight golden ear-hoops on a square of coarse, brightly patterned cloth. Madauc, once recovered from his astonishment, was furious. He looked as if he could very cheerfully have wrung Coala's neck, but the stricken faces of the villagers of Bopillá made him swallow his anger. Whatever tale or threat the girl had used to wring their few treasures from them, it was clear that to refuse the trinkets would dismay, perhaps offend them. What had she said? What was she *saying?* After an alarmed look at Madauc's scowl, she was chattering away again in the harsh language so at odds with her high, clear voice.

All smiles as Madauc scooped up the pathetic little collection of baubles, the villagers of Bopillá promptly struck up their odd, plaintive music and set out for the gate of the town. As Coala and the sullen, supply-laden Companions followed, Madauc—still looking like a thundercloud—slipped the gold ornaments to Dewi and jerked his head toward the empty square behind them.

"Look if there is a temple. Or put them in the largest house, somewhere they're sure to be found," he said grimly.

His errand accomplished, Dewi caught up with them on the banks of the river where a little fleet of long dugout boats clustered along the shore. Coala had very sensibly arranged for the travelers to be ferried upstream to a point on the eastern bank where a well-kept track plunged northeastward through the forest. No sooner were they landed and the boats turned back to Bopillá than the angry prince tried, with many gestures and little success, to make clear to their apparently well-meaning guide just when and from whom one took gold. Coala could only blink and shrug helplessly, and the explanation bogged down when Madauc heard himself roar, "Damnation, we wouldn't be taking a *cartload* of unearned gold unless someone was wishing to put up a fight for it!" This less than fortunate statement fell into a dead silence. Madauc wheeled to glare at Red Kynon. "You were going to say?"

"Why, nothing, my lord." Red Kynon's sandy eyebrows went up. He smiled sweetly and succeeded in looking like the red demon Coala thought him. "It is only that you seem to have left a small something in Bopillá." He pointed.

A boy Dewi's age, clad only in a loincloth and stripes of yellow paint, passed up the line of men stretched out on the dark, narrow trail. He carried a small cloth package, and with a deep bow he handed it over, turned, and was gone.

Coala peered around Madauc's shoulder as he unwrapped it. The pin and earrings lay in his palm. When he looked up, she had whisked away and was hurrying along the trail. The Companions followed.

"I'd beat the vixen if I thought she would be knowing what it was for," Madauc muttered.

* * *

Two days later, at sunset, Coala brought them to a thinly wooded hillside and showed them a great city in the valley below. She had brought them skirting around to the east of it. Gleaming white and gold in the sun, it bewildered and astonished them. "City" meant to them walled Conwy or Degannwy; only Red Kynon had once seen Llundain, the great town of England. Tushcloshán was not so large or crowded as that, but it was splendid and far larger than all of the sizable towns of Gwynet together. It sprawled across the river plain: broad streets lined with steep-roofed detached houses, large and small, radiating from a tall flat-topped mound in the city's center, an artificial hill crowned by a golden temple.

The Companions were angered that the barbarian girl should have led them in a wide circle around this first of the seven cities, but their anger was quickly lost in excitement. There was no doubt that this was one of the legendary cities of Antillia. *This* was what they had come for, not for a misty, mythical Avallach-Abalóc, a magical island that held no reality outside of the old tales of Artair and Margan spun by old women and bards. Here was gold!

Their elation was short-lived. Prince Madauc was first among them to recover from that confusion of amazement and desire and to look more sharply at the defenses of the great wall surrounding the city and at the activity in the city itself. Silencing his men with a harsh command, he announced tersely that to march under arms into such a city was impossible, and even the swiftest raid through an unguarded gate sheer madness. They had only to wipe the dazzle of gold from their eyes. Even at this distance they could make out companies of soldiers wearing plumed headdressses and bearing brightly decorated shields, drilling in several of the broad plazas. If the village of Bopillá had made them feel no better than brigands, this was disturbing in quite another way.

The men cursed Fortune and Antillia, Coala, and each other. Several, close to tears with rage and baulked desire, vowed they would stay where they were and go in over the wall that night after the moon was down. Through all the turmoil Coala waited impassively, as if to say, "You may please yourselves. Go into the city if you will, or you may follow me." Madauc watched her narrowly, as if trying to divine what obscure plans might be hidden behind those calm, dark eyes. For a moment he looked at the city thoughtfully, pondering its preparations for war, and then turned his back on it. Gesturing to the girl to lead the way, he took up Tochtlú and followed her over the brow of the hill and into the forest.

Madauc had the measure of his men. Had he stopped to argue or moved them on with threats and orders, blood might have been shed. Instead, uncertainty and a secret fear of this strange land that might well, for all they knew, *be* on the edge of Faerie, drew them, reluctant, after the determined figure of their captain.

Traveling east into hilly country, northeast through a long, broad valley, they came after some days into a high country of river, rising bluffs, waterfall, and mountain ridge. The forest was cool and quiet, more light and open than the dank lowland jungles. Great magnolias, slippery elms, and silver bell and liquidambar trees climbed the hillsides; ferns and yellow violets grew in the hollows and on the slopes among the mountain laurels and camellias. There were neither settlements nor trails, yet if Coala were rightly understood, the city of Etowán was no more than two days' journey to the east. Further upstream along the river that was their guide, the Companions found a ledge—two feet wide in some places and at no point more than five—which climbed the high, narrow bluff around whose foot the river bent as it came down from the waterfall beyond. The file of men went up between two great rocks onto the high arm of land and made camp with Cibotlán stretching away at their feet.

Such a land and so empty! The men marveled.

Madauc disappeared with those who went off after game. He came back just before dark, abstracted, in a strange mood. "A commander with thirty men could hold this point against an army," he announced to no one in particular. "The ledge is the only way up, and an outpost below the rocks would make surprise impossible. Think of a fortress like Dolwydlan here!"

"Ah, we'll be thinking of it where it is," said one disgruntled soul, voicing the feeling that stirred in some of them. "Or better yet, no fortress, but a hill farm and a sweet soft girl to wife." There were murmurs of agreement.

"Oh, aye!" Red Kynon laughed. "But with your face, Tryffin, you'll be doing better with a little gold in your purse and a string of pearls to dangle in front of this soft little bird you're thinking of."

It was not the wisest of remarks. The lost, but not forgotten, splendor of the temple of Tushcloshán glittered in Tryffin's eyes, and discontent settled over the men like a pall.

Dewi saw Coala flush uncomfortably at the word "gold." She went away from the fire to the bed that had been improvised for little Tochtlú and, wrapping herself in a skin cloak, lay down to sleep beside him. She was a puzzle Dewi worried over, but he did not mistrust her as Madauc seemed sometimes to do. Yet she did behave very strangely toward their captain, jumping at every gesture and hanging anxiously on every—to her—meaningless word. It could be fear, or adoration, or both together. But neither made sense. And what did Madauc himself think of as he paced the perimeter of their high point of land? Of this place? Or of Gwynet? Or of Abáloc?

If we go so far as Abáloc, at least we will have been

there. Abáloc. Avallach. Dewi repeated the name as if it were beyond believing. *But what if we come empty-handed home from Abáloc? Who will believe we've been there? And the oracle. If there ever was an oracle to be lost, who's to say it is still there to be found? And what has it to do with us?* The wordless doubts, the small anxieties that had pricked him had grown to questions, and behind each question was a growing sense that there were answers: out of reach, dark now, perhaps never to be sharp and bright; but answers.

Doubt and silence grew among the others, but the beauty of the land drew them on.

Mountains, rivers; ridge after ridge of deeply forested mountain stretched north and east abreast of them. They traveled a high, rich valley between the ridges until the stream that climbed beside them was no more than a runlet in the wooded uplands. From that point, Coala knew only to strike north. At every questioning she made her sign for "river": a great river. When, on the following day, they came to an open place and saw below them lesser hills rolling away north, and a river running north among them, she laughed and danced, as if surprised that she had led them so true.

The next day saw the company camped on a wooded hill above the stream. All were sore-footed and hungry, and three of the men were too weakened by a persistent fever to go farther. Madauc, understanding certain scratches Coala made in the earth to be a map of this stream as it joined the great river flowing out of Abáloc, decided that they should make coracles. Ten of the skin boats, each large enough to carry four or five men with room to spare, were to be made. Willow frames were bent and lashed, the pitch was gathered, hunting parties came and went, and deer hides were prepared. Coala chafed, but the Companions grew more cheerful as they made up for weeks of short rations; and good meat and broth sped the recovery of those who had weakened and burned with the strange fever. Most were recovered when little Tochtlú fell ill, and in him it burned with a frightening violence. It was four days before Coala would leave his side, and a week before he was playing underfoot again.

Dewi, skilled neither in hunting nor coracle-building, spent most of his days at one of the lookout posts on the hills up and downstream from the steeper hill where the camp was laid out. One morning while Mailcun was out with the hunters as usual, Dewi sat in the high crotch of a great oak tree, idly watching the workers far below who stitched with bone awls and tough leather strings at the coverings on the light boats, and others who coated the finished coracles with pitch. He almost missed seeing a narrow column of men moving stealthily downstream from the southern hills and, for an absentminded moment, watched their progress with no more than a mild interest.

Armed men. Tattooed, most of them: two with elaborate and colorful patterned bands around ankles, knees, wrists,

and elbows. Men coming from the southern hills! Suddenly awake, he nearly fell out of his tree.

"Cor-aaw!" He gave the hoarse cry of a chough and saw the men on the riverbank put down their tools at the signal. Dropping from his perch, he crept to the brow of the hill. The strange warriors moved warily, but they were unprepared for the sight that met them as they came around the bend. The long-haired, bearded men of Gwynet faced the tattooed, bronze-skinned men of Cibotlán in mutual astonishment.

"Hai, Coala!" Dewi grinned as he watched her undignified, sliding descent to the river's bank from the camp above. She had donned her golden regalia hastily and carried her diadem in her hand, but she advanced on the strange soldiers with supreme assurance. She stopped abruptly, with an arrogant lift of the head, and he heard the singsong harshness lash out at the hapless two with elaborate banded tattoos, who seemed to be the officers. Backing a little, they bowed, conferred together, answered her respectfully, and peered curiously upward to see Madauc, little Tochtlú, and Red Kynon watching them. Bowing more violently, they promptly—though not without confusion—turned their men and marched back as they had come.

"Oh!" Dewi whispered, hugging himself with delight. "I should give *any*thing to know what it is she tells everyone that frightens them so witless!"

"*Any*thing?" A voice cut across his silent laughter.

Dewi whirled. A strange young man in a tattered white tunic moved toward him through the trees: a thin young man, smooth-faced, brown-skinned, dark-haired, and blue-eyed. He held a roughly trimmed but wickedly sharp spear and seemed in the grip of some odd excitement. He smiled and, bowing, gave Dewi his answer.

"She says she is priestess to the god who is Winged Man and Serpent. She bids them look on the god and fear, so that he may not speak the death word over them."

"But . . . *what* god?"

The young man looked at him humorously. "Why, the god whose hairs are the sun's rays. The god Matec. Are you not one of his demons?"

Dewi blinked, but alarm rose faster than laughter at Coala's ruse. "How . . . how do you speak our tongue?" he whispered, all in a rush, eying the point of the spear. It did not waver.

The other's blue eyes narrowed. "Nay," he said, very softly. "Rather, how is it that you speak one so like *ours?*"

4
Meeting

"How am I to answer that? I don't even know who you may be," Dewi said, in slow wonder.

"What do you say?" The young man frowned, lowering the spear point a little.

"Who are you? Where do you come from?"

The other ignored his questions. "The accent is strange. On your tongue the words are blurred, and yet musical, and some have odd rhythms that trick the ear when spoken slowly. Do you understand my speech? Or do I walk in a dream?"

Dewi hesitated. "I—I understand, but not clearly. The words are sharp-edged, and you bend them in strange shapes."

Some deep excitement gripped the young man, and he mastered it with an effort, as if he bit back a hundred questions. Swiftly, unexpectedly, he reached out a strong hand to Dewi's elbow, whipping him around, so that the boy stood, with the spear's sharp point pricking in the small of his back, looking out upon the river and the wood across it. The stream was broad and deep enough for small craft, but not so very wide, and above its thickly wooded far bank, where a small rivulet ran down a narrow, grassy hollow, he saw shadowy figures moving parallel to the river. He stiffened and would have cried the alarm if the spear had not given him a prod that made his breath catch painfully.

"Be silent! Do you wish to see the soldiers of Cibotlán back again? We mean your people no harm, but we cannot trust your little golden she-cat, and we have not come such a long and crooked way to be caught four days from home. Your downstream guard will see nothing, for the wood is thick opposite his post, and by the time they find you gone, we will be well away."

The implications of this plan had scarcely dawned on Dewi when the prick was gone and he found his hands tightly bound, whipped around with a length of deer-hide string as neatly as if it had been a piece of conjuring.

"I think you will hold your tongue," the young man said softly, "or your friends will be as dead as mine. Two companies of soldiers from Etowán and Cutivachcó are combing the hills to the south. These you saw were no more than a scouting party, all village militiamen but for the two officers. We have been hounded in circles like hares, and I have no mind to be caught like one. Come!"

"But that means leaving the Companions to them!" Dewi twisted free of his grip and backed away. "What if Coala cannot trick the others?"

"It is no trick," the other said grimly, taking up the spear again. "Her garb and manner tell that much. She is a princess of Cibotlán, and priestess of the Serpent oracle, journeying north, so she says, in search of that accursed oracle that is the root of darkness and all our misery. No northland officer will dare to doubt her power. Come."

With a prod of the sharp point he urged Dewi down the slope and then upstream to a shallow ford, hidden from the camp by the intervening hill.

There were twenty of them: young men and women, boys and girls, some of Dewi's age, one or two younger, and all quite small in stature. Ragged, hungry, graceful, they slipped among the forested hills like a herd of wary young deer and by nightfall had left the river and the Companions' camp long miles to the southwest. The young men in turn carried on their backs three of their number—two girls and the youngest boy—who were flushed and weak with a fever like that which had struck among the Companions. Even so encumbered, they kept to a free, swinging pace that left Dewi dry-mouthed and numb with weariness long before sundown, when they made camp. Only the threat that he would be trussed and carried on a pole stiffened him enough to see the last hour through. Four days more? So they said. But Dewi lay exhausted, too tired almost to eat his small share of roast rabbit and young wild sweet potatoes half baked in the carefully screened little campfire. They would have to carry him to Abáloc!

For it was Abáloc that they made for, straight as an arrow's flight. It was their home. Dewi gathered that Lincoas, the one who had—so easily—made him prisoner, was the leader; and that the little company had been captured by soldiers of Cibotlán some two months past when they were on a hunting trip near the fringes of their own land. Exactly how they had escaped, he could not make out; they had been taken far to the east under heavy guard and were being conveyed to Tushcloshán when under cover of some confusion they had slipped into the hills and over the ridges into the deserted lands. For a long while they had been lost, but the soldiers who searched for them were less mobile and were hindered by the fever that thinned their numbers brutally while causing no more than a painful discomfort to their escaped prisoners.

"We shall make a carrying net for our shamble-footed captive and bear him Cibotlán fashion." A pert, dark-haired girl whose name was Siona grinned at Dewi. "He is too heavy for even Baras to carry on his back, and that way we could go on as fast as ever."

"I would not wish one of those swinging fish baskets on anyone," said another in half rebuke at her teasing.

Dewi spoke stiffly. "It makes little difference. I would have come to Abáloc whether you willed or no; and by a faster way. We were making boats. I have told you."

"So you have," said Lincoas. "But we do not believe you would have come to Abáloc. If the little snake-girl has witched your companions, still we know better. She means to fit you to some purpose of her own. And no good one, I warrant. Oh, she may seek the ancient oracle, but it is not in Abáloc."

"Why not?"

Lincoas stood, stretched wearily, and looked down at him. "Because," he said with a gentle bitterness, "we should know of it if any do. Abáloc was once a great kingdom and held many wonders within its borders. The earth beneath your feet once was Abáloc. Now it is part of the tributary lands of Cibotlán and is deserted, and we are dwindled from a great people and a marvelous city to several hundreds in a village by the great river, all because of the whisperings of this oracle. If it lay among the hills that are the remnant of Abáloc, we should know of it."

"But if it is in Cibotlán," Dewi objected, "why haven't *they* found it?"

The young fugitives exchanged uneasy glances.

"What of—" Siona began.

"Before the Northern Wars Aztlán knew the oracle!" interrupted another. "I have heard the tale my grandfather had from his grandfather. After Aztlán was defeated and before the carrion folk of Cibotlán moved into the seven abandoned cities, it was that same oracle that warned the wise men of Abáloc to abandon the City of the Moon under the Mountain! Some at the time were uneasy and wondered that the wise men should trust its prophecy."

"Aye, but they obeyed. They left the old city and destroyed the old books, and we have been in the hands of the wise men ever since." Lincoas frowned at the speaker. "That is no news."

"Elis means only that the wars in which Aztlán was defeated were fought on the borders of the old Abáloc," Siona urged. "So, if both sides knew the oracle . . ."

"I see. In Abáloc or not, it must have been within reach of the City of the Moon under the Mountain," agreed Lincoas. "But what help is that?"

"I always supposed this oracle was no more than a manner of speaking, a way of saying that a wise man had seen into the heart of some truth," one young man ventured.

While they talked, Dewi had been debating the risk of trying to slip away and make his way back to the river, but something made him listen with a growing fascination. This talk of wars and loss—the oracle—and a folk whose speech was kin to Gwynet's—so that tale of Diermit, the seer, had *not* been of his own making! It was beyond coincidence.

"It would have been to the advantage of the wise men to let the oracle be thought no more than a symbolic way of speaking of their own wisdom," said the one called Baras dryly. "So long as that wisdom was trusted, the place of the oracle could be their secret."

Lincoas was doubtful. "But surely they would have told the kings! Of course they would have! Old Ayacas, for one, would never have kept such knowledge from my father-king Tepollomis. Ayacas cannot *know.*"

"But what of Neolin?" whispered one of the sick girls, raising up shakily on an elbow. "Neolin does not share all of the secrets of the wise with Ayacas."

"Yes, what of Neolin?" chorused several.

Lincoas shook off the question as if it was a challenge he would not meet. "But think! Since the aftermath of the Northern Wars Abáloc has heard no more of oracles.

Might that not mean that the oracle, too, was left behind, somewhere beyond the lost City of the Moon under the Mountain? If it ever really existed."

They spoke so quickly that for a time Dewi lost the train of argument. These "wise men" had apparently led Abáloc from splendor to obscurity, their own power growing as Abáloc's dwindled; and its people knew no more of their own history than what had come down to them in fragments of song and legend. These young people hoped—he could not untangle the whole of it—hoped to recover this lost knowledge and the whereabouts of the lost City of the Moon under the Mountain. It seemed there existed one book, preserved from the long-ago destruction, which they had new hopes of deciphering. The lost city, their lost past, obsessed them.

They had forgotten Dewi altogether and were startled, then rooted in fear and amazement, to hear a clear voice singing out of their own lost past.

"Man folds his wings
To tread the narrowing ring;
The serpent throned devours the circle
And himself.

"Winter's rule is violent,
Summer's song is silent,
The island of the apple trees
Is drowned in war.

"Unknown the oracle's round;
Yet if the lost be found,
And if the fallen spring again,
Then

Stones shall bruise the serpent's head,
And summer's song be sung again!"

Into their silence he dropped the tale Diermit told that had come from his father's grandfather.

"In the days of the Northern Wars!" someone whispered.

Lincoas drew a deep breath and shook off his wonder. Eying Dewi speculatively, he said, "So it is true that you seek Abáloc. That does not change things. Perhaps it is even true that your snake priestess means to take you there, thinking to use your companions as a ruse to disarm us from within. Cibotlán would, I think, give much to see the breaking of Abáloc to harness and to the giving of tribute. *We* were tribute taken, not offered. They search for us as a great prize that has escaped them, but they desire always the greater prize yet; the deeper conquest. They desire as gift the surrender of Abáloc's spirit. Its wealth and lives they could take at any time. Why, if your snake priestess's oracle exists, and if it is the same ill-omened voice that set Abáloc first adrift, what deathly secrets may it whisper in her ear?"

"No, it's not true," Dewi maintained stoutly. "She will do what our captain wants." But secretly he was not at all sure of that.

Lincoas went on thoughtfully, not hearing. "We must stop awakening old evils or bringing new ones upon us. The strange boats your hairy savages were making? They will bring her to Abáloc before us, and that must not be. But tomorrow we reach the end of the deserted lands, at the shore of the Great River, and I do not think they will be there before us."

"Shall we pluck her from the water and carry *her* in a fishnet?" said the youngest with a laugh.

"Aye, and still be home no more than two days past Midsummer."

They looked at Dewi with curiosity, and not unkindly; but as if it all were settled. He shifted uncomfortably, guessing that they had in mind for him the distinctly disagreeable role of the worm that baits the hook. The worst of it was the realization that the Companions would not obligingly stand still for explanations. One threat, one arrow, and they would spring to battle like starving men come to a feast. Their nerves were strung like harp strings; they yearned only for Gwynet, and thought in their hearts that Madauc followed a will-o'-the-wisp. These things, and their resentment at having to live like brigands without any of the rewards of brigandage, had made even the most cheerful of them touchy and spoiling for a fight. The thought of the earnest, gallant gaiety of these young folk pitched against Coala's "demons," the bravest and bloodiest flowers of Gwynet, made him turn his face away from the fire and shiver. Yet how could he prevent it?

Dewi felt doubly drawn to them because they had spoken of a past that was lost, confused, patched up of tales and memories that, strung together, still made no song for the heart to sing and had too little rhyme or reason. Like his own. *Abáloc.* The word's power over his imagination deepened as they told him of the place, of their families and friends. And they had an easiness, an openness, a willingness to delight even on the edge of peril in a bird's evening song or a fat, black-masked *racoan* kit who ambled into the circle around the fire and ignored his mother's insistent hissing to come away. Perhaps there was no gold in Abáloc. There might be other things.

"What if we are kindred?" he said suddenly, turning with an inspiration that might win them at least to caution. "How else can you explain the likeness in our speech? Gwynet is an ancient land, and if you say you know nothing of your past before the old wars, how do you know that *Gwynet* is not your past? What if men from Gwynet came here long ages ago and never got home again? What if they joined with people who were here before them?

That could explain a lot, couldn't it? About the languages, and your skins being darker than ours, and . . . well, *none* of the folk we've seen here in Antillia—or Cibotlán or whatever you call it—have blue eyes, as some of you do, or anything but black hair . . ."

Seeing the indecision that wavered around the circle, he plunged on eagerly. "There are even older stories in our country that must be some dark memory of your Abáloc. Ancient songs and scraps—fairy tales, the learned men say —about a summer island called Avallach. That is why Madauc, why *all* of us," he amended eagerly, "wished to come across the sea: to see if it were true. If you try to take Coala, you make an enemy of Prince Madauc. Even if you aren't all killed, it's scarce worth it."

Lincoas lay back, his hands clasped behind his head, and raised his eyebrows skeptically. "Tell me, do they in your land have old stories of the great wealth of this Avallach?"

Dewi flushed. Even by the light of the tiny, well-screened fire they saw his darkened cheeks and laughed. But it was not an unfriendly laughter. "The drowned woman did have a gown of pearls," he said. "And the man wore this." He held out the talisman and waited expectantly as they examined it.

"It must have some meaning," said Lincoas when the silver disc had gone full circle and come back to him. "But I do not know what it may be. And it traveled across the sea?"

"Prince Madauc thinks the ship must have been swept out upon the ocean in a storm, and the beating of the waves was too much for it."

"Then we have lost more than we know. Our people must have known the sea and sailed it. Yet . . ." He broke off. "Why, my mother, Queen Erilla, has a trinket that reminds me a little of this! It is not the same, but there is writing on hers that may tell us something of both, for if we bring nothing else out of Cibotlán, at least we have learned the secret of the art of writing, which the wise men stole away from us at your oracle's bidding! Hai! Riddle us your riddle again."

They talked for hours, and few had any sleep. They were caught in Dewi's excitement. At the first light the little company was on the move, however, sleep or no. Lincoas did not mean to miss meeting the strange boats that Dewi said were so near ready.

5

The Great River

There was no trace of the boy until Mailcun, coming in with the last of the hunters, caught the scent that led the searchers to the fording place. The trail had grown cold and the going was slow, but Madauc and six others followed the hound until dusk grew thickly among the trees. Then they called him back and made their way to the hilltop camp. Weary and disheartened, they did not notice when Mailcun fell back, turned, and set off through the wood on his own.

At least the boy had not been taken by the barbarian soldiers. But Madauc could not think why he would go off on his own. It was an uneasy omen. It had brought the Companions, Coala even, to a pitch of watchfulness that made them a danger to each other, imagining shadows where there were none. To fight this fear without a source, Madauc, despite his anguish and his responsibility for the boy, had ordered the boats into the water at dawn.

The morning swept them north, and the afternoon saw

them, paddles dipping in a tireless rhythm, on the wide river. *The wide river of the boy's dream,* Madauc thought, and missed his stroke. The girl Coala, cradling little Tochtlú as he slept, saw and reached out timidly. The captain, from the corner of his eye, saw the small brown hand come close and then draw back. The boy had trusted her. Well, perhaps he had been right; but Madauc could not shake the conviction that she had some purpose all her own. Perhaps she sought her man, the child's father, in Abáloc.

The wide river gleamed a silvered blue in the summer sun. Two forests rolled down to the water, the northern as deep and unbroken a green as that to the south. On the banks giant sycamores trailed long branches, fresh with summer green, in the sky-colored water, mile after mile. It was as if the river unrolled beneath them and the coracles stood still. Only an occasional bend, a distinctive hill or tree approaching and falling behind them, showed it was not so. Now and again they saw low, sandy flats stretching along one bank near a bend in the river's course.

"My lord!"

The low-pitched call carried clearly across the water from another of the large coracles, one roughly abreast of Madauc's own and some twenty yards nearer the south bank. Red Kynon signaled, gesturing urgently toward a sandy flat perhaps a quarter of a mile ahead.

"Dewi!" Madauc shipped his paddle and shaded his eyes against the westering sun's glare on the water. A familiar figure stood on the low point of land, waving both arms wildly. A liver-colored hound stood beside him.

"Holy Teilo!" Madauc said. "How does he come to be *here?*"

The man who sat beside him, one Idris of Henryd, pointed. "Captain, look! Beyond. Boats, are they?"

There were boats: a large number of long, shallow-bottomed craft moored under the trees at the inlet of a smaller stream two hundred yards beyond the open flat and out of sight to anyone on the nearer shore. They might have gone unseen even from the water but for a bright orange and red awning on the largest of them.

"Pull!" Madauc called. He grabbed his paddle. The light skin boats skimmed the water.

"Oh, my lord captain," Idris panted after a moment. "I should never have left my poor old mother. Who's to care for her when I'm dead?"

"Don't talk like a fool, man."

"Fool, is it? Only look yonder!"

They were close enough to the shore to see that it was Dewi, and no mistaking, but in a moment everything else was in confusion. A cry went up. Two slim female figures carrying spears sprang down the wooded bank and ran to the spit of land where Dewi stood. At the same moment a massed company of soldiers appeared among the trees: tall men, large and well built, some tattooed as those they had seen the day before, and the others painted all over their bodies with stripes of scarlet, white, yellow, and black. They were plumed and carried shields, and many bore

bright pennons on their spears. They came at a run toward Dewi and the two girls who had joined him, rattling the spears upon their shields and shouting.

It was then, to the surprise of the soldiers as well as the watchers in the boats, that the warriors were assaulted by lances and arrows from within the wood. At the same time, one of the officers of the advancing company caught sight of the little fleet coming up the river. Seeing that they had much more to deal with than three children armed with crude spears, he slowed the advance of his men and gave orders that shaped them into two wings, well covered by their overlapping shields.

Coala, shrieking maledictions or commands that could not be heard on the shore, almost put her foot through the bottom of the hide boat in her anger. Madauc scarcely heard. "*Children?*" he exclaimed. "Who can our Dewi have fallen in with? Girl-children at that, the little devil! Come, men, pull harder. And you in the back, string your bow if you're not on an oar. I mean to get that boy off!"

The Cibotlán patrol was caught in the open between wood and water, between a flight of long arrows and a shower of slingstones. Their officers fell in the first volley, and their lines wavered. Those in the van milled in confusion and in growing terror at the invisibility of the one enemy and the all too visible demons flying across the water in magic vessels, the like of which they had never seen. Dewi and the two girls took advantage of the confusion to wade a little way into the river and help to pull in the boats and steady them as the Companions leaped the bows. With the wild cry of the war band of Gwynet, they drew their swords and splashed into battle as if it were a homecoming. Coala shrieked to no avail and stumbled ashore in a fury to carry Tochtlú, bobbing on her back like a little possum clinging to its mother's fur, to a place out of danger from the flying missiles.

When the young people of Abáloc sprang from under the trees, the soldiers from Cibotlán set up a triumphant howl, and their front ranks rallied and leaped forward, swinging heavy war clubs studded with obsidian blades. The archers behind kept up an unnerving high-paced fire of their short black arrows so that they flew and fell together in dark, dangerous clouds. The Companions fell back momentarily, startled as much by the appearance beyond the soldiers of half-naked allies as small as children as by their own injuries and the rush of the painted warriors.

The struggle was not easily decided; but in the end the victory, if it was to be called that, fell to the strangely met allies. The loss of the splendid officers had shattered the terrifying discipline of Cibotlán, the deadly precision of that wedge of men. Their movements blurred. Their forays grew ragged, indecisive. They struggled, thrashing like a headless snake. At sundown the battle was ended, but only with great loss. Five of the Companions had died and, of the young people of Abáloc, three young men and a girl of sixteen summers. Many more were hurt. Madauc limped up and down in the dusk, commanding those who were unhurt; and before the moon rose, the boats of Cibotlán, which had been hidden under the trees, were a quiet fleet upon the river, laden with the dead, bearing their grim news to Natilchizcó and the sea. The bodies of their own dead they buried under the eaves of the forest. More had died than saw the battle. Near the place where the boats had been moored was found a shallow unfilled grave with the bodies of more than a score of soldiers dead of the now familiar fever, and these they buried as well.

"What is that fool girl moaning about now?" asked Madauc wearily. He leaned against a grassy bank while Dewi held a torch for Red Kynon to see by as he bound up his captain's leg. "I wouldn't half mind setting *her* adrift," Madauc grumbled, "and not just to oblige our new friends. She's madder than the lot of us. Watching and plotting, I warrant. But what for?"

"Who knows? Mmph. I mislike this swelling, Captain. One of those stubby black arrows, was it? Idris is dead of a scratch not much worse than this. Along his ribs, it was. Took him an hour ago." Red Kynon prodded gently. "What does it feel like?"

"Nothing. It throbs, but there's no pain."

Lincoas, a still shadow sitting on the bank above, came down to have a look. "*Tzolát!*" he called harshly to Coala. Signing for her to come close, he put a question to her in her own language, which he repeated twice, with growing impatience. The girl, unhearing, stared uncomprehendingly at Prince Madauc and the bloodstained bandage.

"Was it this sort of arrow?" Lincoas asked Madauc, turning to retrieve one that had lodged in the bank nearby.

"Yes." Madauc nodded wearily.

Coala, bewildered, her gaze sliding again and again from the prince of Abalóc to the astonishing spectacle of an invincible god bleeding like any mortal, listened to Lincoas in growing alarm. In swift answer she made a graphic, slithering motion with her hand. "*Ai, kwutlá!*"

"Viper venom?" Red Kynon sat back on his heels. "You mean those devils poison their cursed arrows with it? But then what are we to do? There's nothing . . ."

Dewi thrust the torch at Red Kynon and knelt beside Madauc. "We should have known an hour ago. Much good it'll do, but there is a trick." The memory sprang from nowhere. "You bind it loosely above the swelling and use a stick to wind it tight so that the poison can't get past."

Lincoas nodded, unsheathing his knife as he watched.

"Good. But slowly, and not so tight as that. Come, don't look so stricken. If he is not dead by now, he is not likely to be. But you may save him a fever and a few days' lameness."

Madauc did not hear. He was tired, and sleep lapped around him—until they hurt him with the knife to make the wound bleed freely. He flinched awake to find Red Kynon holding him down and Dewi looking faintly ill. Lincoas sat on his heels, laughing silently, and Coala was sucking fiercely at the wound. She spat and bent again, and Madauc smiled faintly, too, to see her, for her eyes were angry and the tears fell steadily, splashing down his knee like young waterfalls. Then, sobering, he frowned at the brown-skinned young man who seemed suddenly to find her so entertaining. "It is not so humorous for the wench to see her countrymen die. It is ungentle of us to laugh."

Lincoas grinned. "Ah, but that is not it, you see. I suspect your princess does not in truth *know* why she weeps, but from what she has said, it would seem she is grievously disappointed at this little scratch of yours. You see, my friend, if you can bleed and the snake's milk can make you ill, all her hopes of gaining safety from her enemies are cruelly dashed."

Madauc and Red Kynon stared their puzzlement. Dewi, remembering Lincoas's account of Coala's speech to the officers of Cibotlán the day before, hid a smile. So her "ruse" had been in earnest!

"It is true," Lincoas insisted, mastering his laughter. "Spears should glance from you and arrows turn back upon the bowmen! Above all, snakes should be the best of omens! I think most of all she weeps because she feels very foolish. The folk of Cibotlán are very superstitious, wrapping themselves up in witchcraft and fearful legends of the gods of death. She had taken you, friend Madauc, for some great god whose name of honor is 'Feathered Serpent' and whose priestess she is. It is an old tale of Aztlán, Coala says: that the god was yellow-haired and tall and that he sailed eastward on the sea one day in the Third Age—that would be thousands of years ago—after promising to return again."

The Companions crowded around and roared with delight as the story was repeated. The doctoring finished, Coala stalked off in resentful, injured dignity, looking despite it so forlorn that their merriment withered into an embarrassed silence.

"So that's why she tried so hard to please." Bemused, Madauc watched her disappear into the night shadows beyond the flickering light of the campfires. "I suspected she might be using us for a guard to get her to Abáloc. I guessed she might be out of favor with her own people—that the child's father might be from your country and that she fled to join him. This explains much more."

"No, no, the little boy is her *brother,* Lord Madauc." The girl Siona, who had come unnoticed and sat just behind Dewi, spoke up unexpectedly. Ignoring the swift, sharply curious look Madauc turned upon her, she addressed Lincoas excitedly. "Their mother was a great princess, sister to the Seven Kings of Cibotlán—but she is dead now, and their father, too. Oh, my lord, Coala and the little one *must* come with us to Abáloc. She has told me that the priests were to sacrifice Tochtlú in our place if we were not recaptured and brought to Tushcloshán in time for the feast of the god of the Burning Lake. That is why she ran away and left her slaves to say she and the child were sick abed with the fever and like to die."

"The girl is shrewd." Lincoas nodded appreciatively. To Madauc he explained, "There is nothing Cibotlán fears so much as this dark fever. They call it 'The God's Anger,' and the last time they were plagued by it, it is said a hundred thousand died. Aye, your Coala is shrewd. But indeed I mislike the shrewdness that comes out of Cibotlán and would not have it poison Abáloc."

"B—but the child . . ." Siona faltered. "He would have died in our place. Is it not too wondrous for chance that we have been bound together in this way beyond our knowing? How can we . . ."

"My lord?" Dewi interrupted. His eyes gleamed in the firelight. "We are all tied in even stranger ways." To Madauc and his Companions he poured out what he had heard of Abáloc and the oracle and the Northern Wars, of the lost City of the Moon under the Mountain, and of the book that was hidden in Abáloc that no one had been able to read for more than a hundred years. "But in Cibotlán Prince Lincoas and his followers have learned the key to the old letters, my lord, and wouldn't it be a marvel if they read in the secret *Book of the Kings* that they are our own kindred in some distant way?" He caught his breath. "And Coala is in it, too, because she is the priestess of Diermit's oracle, which is truly lost! She *must* come with us. If we could find it . . ."

Madauc began to laugh softly, shaking his head. "The world is truly upside down," he said when he had caught his breath. "When I believed in wonders, I never saw a one. Now here we are, greedy to make our fortunes, so that we can buy peace and power and honor after the world's way, and we find ourselves instead walking in forgotten legends. I begin to think Llywarch Prydyt y Moch is the wisest of all men! Certainly, if you fix your heart on something beyond what the moment offers, you bind yourself on Fortune's wheel. Think how Lady Fortune must be laughing at the fool who thought he charted his own course!"

Dewi did not know how to answer him. It was as if Prince Madauc would be content with nothing but bitterness after all. . . . It was too confusing. So he thought instead of tomorrow.

III
ABÁLOC

1
Abáloc

They made no camp that night. Crowding the boats a little, they set off upstream, leaving the deserted lands behind and passing King Tulal's Tucrikán, the last of the seven cities, like silent water-shadows in the dark of the moon. And so they came at dawn on the morning of Midsummer to Abáloc, and as the boats swung toward the shore, the young people sang a dawn song that rang among the hills with all their joy at coming home.

For a moment it seemed they heard an answering cry, but on coming to land, they found the quay deserted. Lincoas's call echoed among the trees and across the pale water to the wooded island that slumbered in midstream like the islands in Dewi's old dream. Dewi shivered and ran after the others through the sycamore flats and up into the last stronghold of the kingdom of Abáloc.

It was neither city nor kingdom, stronghold nor seat of power. Seeing it, any of the men of Gwynet who had dreamed of gold did so no longer. A wind not so high as a sea hurricane would have erased it utterly, and yet the memory of it need never grow dim to its people, for it was a garden and could be planted again or made to grow in another place. Flights of small green parrots, yellow-headed, with wings touched with orange and yellow, wheeled among the trees. Flowers bloomed everywhere—along the paths, around the houses woven of willow and roofed and curtained with deer hide. Lincoas called repeatedly and had no answer but the cries of the birds.

At his direction the wounded of the two companies were taken to a large lodge with comfortable beds, while the others searched for some sign of the inhabitants. A rack of venison strips was found hung for curing over a dead fire of hickory wood; a flute half carved from a deer's tibia lay at the edge of a fire circle beside the maker's knife; a downy white mantle lay in the dust by a basket of swans' feathers at the doorway of a pleasant lodge; and rabbits, interrupted in their unaccustomed feasting, fled from the herb gardens and neat plots of flourishing tomato and sweet potato plants. Along the mossy banks of one of the clear pools of a stream that spilled down from the highlands, wooden plates and dishes waited to be washed.

"Something is wrong," said Lincoas when the searchers met at the house highest on the hill. "Last night they ate and turned to evening tasks, and then were called away. There is no sign of hurry or of violence. But where could they go?"

"It will be Neolin's work," said the young man called Baras.

"Aye, it smells of him. He would pipe them over the hills and dance them into Tucrikán if he could." To the prince of Gwynet he explained, "This is the wise man we have told you of. It is power he hungers for, and Abáloc has little of that to offer. We have heard it whispered in Cibotlán that he would sell our hearts and bodies for a crown. I cannot believe he is such a fool, though, to think the kings would give him one." He shook himself, as if to free himself of a fearful mood. "The air is heavy, as if it is some doom come upon us and no dawn."

Coala knelt in the uncomfortable silence and leaned forward to press her ear against the ground. "Drumming," she said to Lincoas in her own tongue, then "*Taramtan* . . . opp by hillss."

Madauc looked at her sharply. "What's up by the hills?

Drums?" He knelt to listen for himself. "She's right. There is some great movement a mile away, perhaps two." He pushed himself up clumsily, favoring the stiff knee. "Well, lads, we must have a look, I think. Doom or dawn, we've come too far to turn away."

"Prince Lincoas!"

The cry was breathless. The dwindled company stared upward through the trees where the last shadows of night still sheltered. Along the course of the falling stream, ignoring the trail that doubled down more gradually, a small boy plunged from rock to rock, panting, almost speechless, his legs scraped from tumbles.

"Oh, please come hurry, Prince Lincoas!" The child stopped above them on the hillside, a doubtful eye on the strange curly-headed men in their ragtag garb, and would come no farther. "Ayacas and the queen say you must come quickly before the Seven Kings come, and Neolin says they mean to take King Amalahtis for a hostage, and he says it wasn't you in the strange boats at all, but soldiers from Natilchizcó, and Queen Erilla is afraid of him, but she sent me anyway . . ."

"Enough, enough!" Lincoas was past him, and the others were close behind.

The wood opened out onto a grassy field below the hill's crest: a shadowy field, its brow crowned with the gold of the sunrise. The small boy trotted alongside the young people of Abáloc, wondering at their thinness, their tattered clothing and makeshift spears, the plaited cotton slings that hung from their belts, and the grim sureness of their haste. The men of Gwynet came behind, a little winded, wondering at everything they saw as they climbed up through the shadowy grass into the morning. The hilltop was covered with people, and a long, low mound of raw earth stretched along its crest. At the mound's center, on a wide platform built up of stones and earth, stood a massive stone altar; and behind it had been raised the first pillars of a temple. A tallish dark man stood before the altar speaking in a high singsong voice, and the crowd milled restlessly but seemed unable to shake free of the droning chant, the rapt, blind-eyed intensity of the man, and the trance he wove.

"No!" some cried. "Give our Lord Amalahtis and our sons and daughters to the Seven Kings? It is unspeakable!" And one said in a strong voice, "What is that but a darker death for us—the death of our hearts?" But most only wrung their hands and drifted helplessly. Many did not notice Lincoas and his companions until they came pushing into the crowd.

"Lincoas! Oh, my son!" A handsome, dark-haired woman in a blue gown flew to him and held him fast. "Oh, my dear, my dear! So many weeks we've thought you—all of you—lost to us. And now we are like to be lost together!" It was as if a dam had broken, as if some long restraint had snapped, for she could not stop the flood of tears. "Oh, *please* do something to stop Neolin! He has persuaded your brother to surrender himself to the kings, and Ayacas is too old and ill to withstand them."

Dewi, standing closest to the mound of any of the Companions, was watching the slow reaction of unbelief of the man who stood above, steadying himself in his uncertainty against the great altar stone.

"That is Neolin," whispered Siona, who had slipped close. "He backs away as if he wished for a good hole to crawl into."

"Like a snake," Dewi agreed. The remark was made in a whisper, but the heavy-lidded black eyes sought and met his own as if the priest or wise man, whatever he was, had heard. Dewi shrank back under the searching gaze, but the

eyes had a compelling power, and he could not turn his own away. He had a frightening conviction that this Neolin groped in the darkness of his memory, turned over his thoughts, measured even the scar on his cheek, and promised to remember him. It was a part of the man's great skill that he could seem to do this and muddy men's minds with doubt. Dewi, on his part, saw with an unwilling fascination a thin, dark man with long, stringy black hair, which glistened as if it were dressed with oil, and clad in a dirty white robe bordered with orange and yellow. He had long, nervous fingers and the eyes of a snake toying with a bird. Dewi was held until the man turned away. Trembling, the boy found Siona still beside him, watching anxiously.

"Neolin has not seen your tall prince," she whispered. "Or the red-haired one. They are keeping out of sight. Perhaps they are standing in some hollow of the ground or sitting hidden by the crowd. The barbarian girl is gone, too. Look there. Do you see the young man by Lincoas who wears a gold circlet on his brow? That is Amalahtis, his brother and our king. Their father, King Tepollomis, was killed in the raid when we were captured and taken away to Cibotlán. The old man in white who leans on the girl in brown? He is Ayacas, the counselor."

The voices of the brothers carried across the silent crowd.

"What is this foolery, brother?" Lincoas demanded. "This mound? And this stone! It is like the altars of sacrifice in Cibotlán. What are such things doing on the Field of Morning? Have we come safely home only to find the same abominations we fled in the south?"

His brother spread out his hands. His eyes were wide, darkened, as if he struggled under the weight of a heavy spell or some burden of the spirit. "No, you are wrong, Lincoas. You do not know . . . you cannot! But it is a great blessing that you were seen upon the river, else we had come close to doing what I cannot think good. . . ." He passed a hand across his eyes. "No, it is cowardly of me to put it so gently! We meant a great evil. Neolin brought a foreign child here as sacrifice to bind us to Cibotlán, to save us from a war we could not hope to survive. Happily the child is gone, escaped—I-I am not sure yet what happened—during the confusion when we saw the strange boats upon the river. But what of the boats? And of these men? What does it all mean?"

"And I would ask the same!"

Neolin, his shaken assurance mended, moved forward from the temple pillars to the mound's edge. Abandoning his former passionate and hypnotic appeal, he spoke in the anguished tones of a man who has been strained to the utmost and seen all his best efforts rejected. "Do you bring a handful of ragged allies and hope to save us from the hordes of Cibotlán, Lord Lincoas? For it *is* war they promise us this day. Do you think I would have counseled desperate remedies if that desperation were not founded in the deepest danger? Yes, I say offer one to save many! The queen, your mother, has never been my friend, but she will tell you: Cibotlán is no longer content to see the upper reaches of the river under our control. They have moved against us. It is their drums you hear. The kings mean to celebrate their Feast of the Burning Lake with the tears of Abáloc. But if you can speak the word that will rout them, or if you have some new choice to offer, why, Neolin is yours to command." A bleak gentleness tinged his voice, masking the insolence that underlay the challenge.

"I fear it is true," said Queen Erilla in a low, unhappy tone as she turned back to them, having given directions that the ailing Ayacas be taken down to the village despite his protests. "You come so late, and your friends are too few. We are worn down, and they are so many."

"But I *do* offer another choice if only we can win the time to take it. My mother, listen!" Holding her eyes with his own, he touched the bronze medallion that hung on her breast. It was engraved and inlaid in silver with a band of strange signs circling an odd shape intended for a tree, for fruit hung from its branching arms. "Shall I read to you the inscription on this ancient sign you wear? Shall I read the figures Neolin holds must be meaningless to all but himself?" He looked defiantly at the man on the mound. "I say to Neolin that it is inscribed with the name *Alida*, and it says, '*Ur men berenina o'r dunum o'r plagro tan'e menet:* in the old tongue, 'For my queen of the City of the Moon under the Mountain.' "

Erilla's hands flew to her mouth in astonishment, and she stared at her younger son in unbelief. Was the deep suspicion that she and the queens before her had held true then? Were the magical signs not spells that, as Neolin claimed, it was dangerous folly to release? From her grandmother's grandmother they had passed down through their daughters the ancient pendant and the only one of the forbidden books brought out of the city against the command of the wise men. But Erilla had no daughter, and she had despaired that the meaning of the letters would ever be recovered. She had not told her sons of the book's existence.

The young king Amalahtis was fully wakened from his trancelike lethargy. He sensed in his brother a deeper excitement than could be explained by an inscription on an old medallion. Neolin, thinking the same, drew in his breath sharply, and his dark skin was suddenly ashen.

"It is impossible," he breathed.

Lincoas ignored him. "We learned the meaning of these signs . . . in Cibotlán. But that is too long a tale for here and how. What else we learned there is that there still may be in Abáloc one of the ancient *Books of the Kings,* and in that book may be a map. If we can win the time to find and read it, what is to stop us from abandoning this place to the Seven Kings and seeking the safety of the lost city, the great fortress of Abáloc-that-was?"

"You are a worse-than-fool to waste precious time on talk of dreams," Neolin hissed. "Not even *I* know where the city was. And what is this 'book' you speak of? Where is it? We all know that all of the magic writings were destroyed when our forefathers set out on their wanderings. The Serpent himself has told me of these things. They were all spells and curses made by the witches of those days to enchant and ensnare the minds of men and draw them away from the rulings of wisdom! *Book of the Kings?* There never were such things, and if there were, they would still be forbidden. Forbidden, rash prince! The making and reading of signs is an art of deep magic and reserved to the wise alone. There is no book. You do an evil thing to raise hopes where there can be no hope. If you think to find refuge in the City of the Moon, you are *all* dreamers, turning your faces from life toward certain doom." His voice rose until it was almost a shriek.

"No, *no*. It is *not* foolishness," whispered Erilla. She clutched at the pendant she wore, running her fingers along the words. "I have such a book. We have kept it hidden all these years: my mother before me and her grandmother's mother before that. I came near to burying it with Tepollomis, my husband, for I thought the key to unlock the letters was utterly lost."

Her words, and a confused rumor to the effect that the legendary citadel of Abáloc had been found, swept through the crowd. Erilla herself seemed in a daze, all danger forgotten.

"Come down with me," she said. "I will show you."

Neolin's upflung arms restrained them. He shook. "One moment, my queen. You have not let Prince Lincoas see how little time is left you! Come, my prince, and all your ragtag company. Come stand where I stand and look you out across the hills. Neolin leaves you to the joy of what you see!" Trembling with frustration and contempt, he whirled and disappeared down the opposite side of the mound.

The folk of Abáloc, snatching at hope however fragile it might be, streamed down through the bright morning grass after Erilla. Lincoas and some of his comrades, and the Companions of Prince Madauc, climbed the face of the long, narrow hillock that crowned the hilltop. Dewi and Siona were among the first. Coala and several others appeared from nowhere and came with Madauc and Red Kynon, who had cannily kept hidden within the trees below, where they could hear much and not be seen.

From the mound's crest Neolin could be seen disappearing into the fold of a shallow valley lapped with woods. Beyond, orchards, fields, and forest, as far as the rolling hills along the sky to the east and south, rippled with color. Banners and robes and feathers of yellow, orange, vermilion, and purple shimmered in the fields of maize and glinted deep in the forest clearings. The closest soldiers were not two miles away; and the heaviest concentration, a massed army in itself, flowed across a green field like molten gold, an unforgettable sight. The splendid tide of bright pennons and armor, shields and plumes, rolled slowly and surely nearer.

Coala watched for a moment impassively, then spoke in a small, cheerless voice. Lincoas turned to Madauc. "Coala says it is all the armies of Cibotlán, and the Seven Kings, and that it is an evil omen that they should come on this of all days, when the great feast is meant to be celebrated in all of the seven cities. I myself and little Tochtlú were their Chosen Ones, and it seems that since we and my companions have escaped that other celebration in which we were to die, they bring the feast to Abáloc. Neolin spoke the truth for once."

"And what of your wizard-friend?" said Madauc. "What will he do? There is no tool so useless to a king as a failed traitor, turned off by the people he would have betrayed. But it looks to me as if he means to salvage something from the ruin."

"Aye," Red Kynon rumbled. "His kind are never behindhand in saving their own skins, never minding the cost."

The golden horde wavered, slowed, and stopped at the edge of the distant field.

"You may be right." Lincoas shaded his eyes against the climbing sun. "They have seen him. The pennons dip. It is a sign they grant him safe conduct for a parley. Ha, Neolin will grind his teeth at that. It is the formal greeting for a suppliant enemy!"

Madauc rubbed his short, curling growth of beard thoughtfully. "Am I right in thinking they would have no boats nearer than Tucrikán? But you have boats. What is to stop your people from taking to the river and finding shelter somewhere upstream on the opposite bank? It would gain you a little of the time you want—time enough at least to see whether this book you speak of is no fairy tale, with its maps and its lost cities."

Lincoas nodded. He wasted no time in reply, but immediately sent down to his brother in the village below the youngest of his followers, along with Maia, the one of them he thought most capable of unriddling the ancient writing of Queen Erilla's book. "Tell King Amalahtis he must take the sick and wounded with him. We will follow when we can."

Madauc all this time paced the mound. He still limped slightly, but the long hours without sleep were forgotten, and something like his old, slow grin came back to make his blue eyes dance. "I think," he said, "that Gwynet must have a hand in this. I wish to heaven Prydyt y Moch were here! It is just the sort of pinch that would gladden his devious soul, and I have been puzzling what he might do." He laughed. "Shall we take a lesson from Llywarch and little Coala here and see if there is more to be won than time? It seems there are other ways of fighting than with blades. As for the risk—we came for gold, and there it is. Ransom enough for seven kings. What says Gwynet?"

With an eye for the distant glint of gold and hearts that rose in delight at the thought of such high trickery, such a deep gamble, the Companions answered "Aye" to a man.

Madauc turned to Lincoas. "Then shall we attend your friend of the snake eyes in his parley? What do you think he will say to finding prince and priestess, demons, and a god in his train? There is a chance that may win us more even than time and gold . . ."

2

The Coming of the God

The hilltop rang with sudden laughter. Coala, when it was explained to her, smiled until the petals of the blue flower on her cheek crinkled, and her laugh rang out like a peal of silver bells. "Yess," she cried, and then in a burst of her harsh, commanding chatter she sent the last of the young people of Abáloc streaming down to the village on urgent errands, Lincoas among them. By signs she ordered the Companions to strip off their tattered boots and robes. "Musst s-show moonsskin," she pronounced, struggling with the sounds. "Ve'y coorious sskin."

Dewi saw Madauc look at her with amusement and respect and not a little surprised concern, as if he would like to send her down to the boats, to join little Tochtlú. But that was impossible. Still, something of the old Madauc seemed alive again. Gwynet was forgotten—for now. The boys and girls of Abáloc came struggling, panting up out of the climbing wood into the steep field. The younger ones came with their arms heaped high with bright feathered garments, and the older ones came in pairs, carrying large baskets between them.

"Queek! Be *huanón?* Yess, be splentid!" Coala clapped her hands in command, and snatching her sack, which Siona had brought, she set about being splendid herself.

Neolin met the kings at the stream called Deep, which ran in a narrow cleft almost hidden in the grass that bordered the orchards of wild sweet crabapple trees. They offered him no cherry wine or cakes. That was the customary greeting for friend or envoy, but they did not offer it. Nevertheless, Neolin boldly stepped across the Deep and knelt to touch his forehead to King Quanohtsín's golden sandals. It was the gesture of submission made by a servant confident of the worth of his service, but the Brother of the Sun did not touch Neolin with the yellow-feathered staff of gold. When this sign of welcome was not forthcoming, the wise man of Abáloc did not dare look up. So he was to keep his head bowed, was he? Anger at the mulishness of those who had earned him this humiliation burned in his throat. He fixed his eyes on the golden sandals of the king and the tattooed green and purple vines and serpents that writhed around his ankles. Those sandals would be on his neck if his wits failed him.

"My lord kings," he cried in the dust, "the sacrifice of the foreign child you sent to me is offered up, consumed by the Sun at dawning. My people are frightened at their own deed and would deny its significance. Yet all will be well."

"How can this be?" The voice was sharp and sibilant. "We saw no signal. Our spies have watched the altar place and seen no fire. A feast for the Sun without fire? My brother kings would have it, Neolin, that you have failed your promise. The folk of Abáloc, they say, are stiff-necked as ever and will never render up the free tribute of lives that is the highest recognition of our power. Can this be so? It would grieve me sorely if it were. No, no, I have told my brother Suns Neolin is too golden-tongued to fail!"

"Ah, my lord Quanohtsín knows his servant Neolin." But the touch of the golden staff did not come.

"Yes." The soft voice flickered. "Too golden-tongued. Double-tongued, perhaps, deceitful. I have told my brothers that Neolin would sooner double-deal than fail. What have they offered you to lie to us? Such fools!"

"No, no. It is not true, Lord Quanohtsín!" Neolin's mind raced in circles like a squirrel in a cage. He snatched at a slender chance. He rubbed his forehead on the ground, and his voice deepened, becoming a breathy groan of sound. "The sacrifice was made, was consumed in a great marvel. The Sun Serpent himself moved in me. He moved in me and I saw the child swallowed by a dark cloud, the darkness of the maw of the Sun himself. The folk of Abáloc were struck with wonder and confusion, but I . . . I was filled with the spirit of the god, and his voice spoke in me, revealing to me the center of things. But those are secrets not to be spoken of. When he left me, the time appointed for the signal was past. I have hastened here in obedience to him, to reveal his new purpose."

There was a strange pause before Quanohtsín answered. Neolin heard the drums cease, but still did not dare to raise his head.

"Take care, Neolin of Abáloc, that it is the god you speak for!" Quanohtsín's voice was almost a whisper. "The god has a heavy hand."

"My lord, do I not know?" The wise man's voice had an unexpected ring of truth. "I have listened to his voice since I was a child, and my grandfather before me, and his father." He paused, then went on more craftily, more cautiously. "The wise men of Abáloc have been favored in this, for they have kept the place of the god's voice since the days of the defeat of Aztlán, long before Cibotlán grew to fill the cities abandoned by Aztlán. It is because of this long service that the Sun Serpent wished his priest Neolin spared to him. All the rest of Abáloc may—"

"Take care, Neolin!" warned the voice of Setsek, another of the kings. The warning held both a hint of fear and much spite.

Neolin hesitated, sensing this, and he was startled, too, by the sound of bells and wind. It was almost as if a great sigh rose from the host of Cibotlán. *Superstitious fools,* he thought. But then he felt a stab of misgiving. How much did they know—how much *could* they know of the ancient oracle of Aztlán? He was sure no one knew beside himself.

He began again, "All the rest of Abáloc . . . "

"Hear this, lords! The god himself will answer for the safety of Abáloc."

The voice was high, half a chant, imperious, completely unexpected: a woman. With the host of Cibotlán? Neolin felt the heavy pressure of the golden staff upon his neck and in a moment had risen, whirling to search out the owner of the voice that dared to speak for the god. He could hear the beating of his own blood in his ears. Who dared to speak for the god? *His* god, his Serpent. The voice of the Serpent had promised him power: power over Abáloc, and all of Cibotlán to follow. He was the god's and the god was *his.*

Then Neolin saw what the kings had seen long minutes before and what had driven the field of men back in awe. He did not understand. He could not seem to take it in. Standing before the orchard, gleaming against its green shadows, stood a golden princess of Cibotlán in the regalia of the Serpent god, golden snakes on her limbs, on her forehead the sign of the god, the Endless One, the Snake Who Swallows Himself. At her side stood the prince of Abáloc and ten of his companions, lithe and brown, clad in

short blue tunics and the blue-and-green feather cloaks of princes. They were unarmed, but terrifying and beautiful in their youth, and they wore pearls upon their brows. They laughed at his confusion, and he could not understand why they laughed when they should tremble. And then he saw.

The god strode out from under the orchard's eaves, out of shadow into the golden sunlight. Taller than any mortal man, he towered, golden-haired, golden-skinned, in a shimmering cloak of white feathers, a wide collar of pearls upon his breast and ropes of pearls around his waist. In his right hand he held—as lightly as if it were pearl or feather—a long, broad glinting blade that caught the dancing sun and stabbed at Neolin's already dazzled eyes. The oth-

ers with him—wild, dark-haired men with golden skin and moon-eyes like the god's—watched him with an ill-concealed eagerness. One or two of the cursed striplings of Abáloc had such gray-blue piercing eyes as that. His own eyes narrowed. These demons . . . he had seen strangers something like them in the crowd on the Field of Morning. He remembered the boy clearly now. He had been in rags then, not in a white tunic stitched with pearls and holding a huge liver-colored hound on a golden chain. *Not with the symbol of the oracle a silver glint on his breast.*

"It is a trick!" Neolin screeched. "It—" At a threatening sign from Quanohtsín he fell silent.

The Seven Kings, their tattooed faces enigmatic, waited. Nothing was clear to them but their contempt for the wise man who had known neither his people nor the foolishness of his own deceits a moment past. They did not see how the sharp eyes of their niece Coala—Coala who had died of the fever and was now a ghost honored by the Sun—how her eyes searched their faces and the ranks of officers behind them.

"Uncles, the god's priestess is commanded to greet you," said the seeming ghost in a peculiar high chant that carried far in the clear air. "The god asks if all of Cibotlán is assembled here."

The kings Quanohtsín, Ititlán, Malinl and T'zomoc, Tulal, Setsek, and Lopán exchanged uneasy glances. Quanohtsín was the first to speak. "We—we had not thought to see you again, niece."

Her eyes gleamed. "My return is commanded. What is your answer, my lords?"

Ititlán replied hastily for them all. "Aye, the whole of our force is here but for two companies long overdue from Natilchizcó."

"We know of them." She brushed the air with her hand as if all of that great host could be brushed aside as easily. "They crossed our path upon the Great River and defied us. For this they have felt the god's curse bitterly, and there is no man of them alive." Seeing that this caught them a little off balance, she raised her arms to intone, "Natilchizcó feels it too, and Tushcloshán, Etowán, Cutivachcó, and Ranoacán are laid waste. Quaunatilcó weeps. Yester eve the curse came to Tucrikán, and this day it comes to you!"

Lincoas darted a nervous, sideways look of alarm at her, but fortunately no one noticed. The kings had eyes only for the frowning brow and piercing glance of the god. They had never in their secret hearts thought to see that tall, golden figure walking out of the old tales onto the green grass of the Middle Kingdoms.

"What curse is this you say we have brought upon us, niece? And why? Where have we offended?" said Setsek, half fearing that he already knew the answer to his first question.

Coala's arms reached out, pointing, the gold snakes gleaming. "What curse? You must ask my uncle Malinl. He feels it. And Tamak among the captains stands in its shadow. Many others, too. Those in the front rank, there and there. They feel the fire in their armpits, and the red spots that grow beneath their golden breastplates, and they feel the dryness that rims their eyes with red. By nightfall tomorrow evening a full tithe of Cibotlán will lie dead upon these hills, for did you not wish to celebrate the feast with death? Each day you tarry here you will pay a tithe, until you are no more. Unless . . . " Coala faltered, and for a moment she became a frightened girl and no ghost-priestess, for as she spoke, a strangled cry came from among the captains. Perhaps it was as much from fear as from the fever, but Tamak the captain dropped his shield and fell senseless in the trampled maize. Taking hold of herself, the princess of Cibotlán spoke to her uncle Quanohtsín, the High King. "This is a cursed place for Cibotlán. Because of your pride, you wished not to destroy Abáloc, but to have Abáloc offer itself to you in tribute. The god bids me tell you *He* is no such fool. His power is no greater for your submission than for your defeat. He says, 'Stay and die if you will.' " With a nod she turned, and the god and his strange company disappeared among the apple trees like so many apparitions.

The noise and confusion swelled. Everywhere men saw or imagined, on themselves or others, the signs of the dreaded fever that had from time to time scourged Cibotlán. "*The God's Anger! The God's Anger!*" they cried. The kings wrangled among themselves. Etowán, Ranoacán, Tushcloshán . . . all waste? The panic spread, and because there was no agreement among the kings, the panic ruled instead. The press increased, and where one turned to flee, ten followed, trampling the less fortunate in the way.

"Come back! It is only some trick! It is some trick!" Neolin screamed as he stumbled after the unhearing kings. Horrified, he looked down to see that he had tripped over the spear of the fallen Tamak, who lay with arms upflung so that the telltale red splotches showed. Neolin whimpered. "It must be some trick," he whispered. "That was not the god. The god would not serve me so. I must seek him out. He will tell me. He will tell me what to do." Turning around and around in a wild, aimless fashion, seeing at last that he was abandoned, the wise man fled from the trampled field, going in a wide circle toward the river so that he would pass well to the north of the village of Abáloc.

Dewi and Siona crouched in the orchard beside the dog Mailcun. "He *does* know where the oracle is," Dewi said. "You heard him back on the mound when he said, 'The Serpent himself has told me'? He's got to be haring off to that oracle or whatever-it-is right now. There's no time to tell the others. Will you come?"

Frightened, Siona nodded.

They ran among the apple trees like flickering shadows, following the silent dog through the green and golden light.

3

The Island of the Apple Trees

"But we do not go to the island," Siona whispered. She drew back as Dewi, at the water's edge, offered a hand to help her down the steep bank. "No one goes to the island." She stared, perplexed, after the hunched figure in the dugout pulling like a madman for the wooded island's northern tip.

"Neolin does," said Dewi dryly. "Do you mean it's forbidden?"

"No-o. At least, I've never heard it *said* that we mustn't go. But islands are . . . *strange*. Don't you think so? I always think they look as if they might draw their cloaks about them and sail off downstream once you set foot on them. Neolin says . . . "

"I thought that might be it," Dewi said with fine scorn. "What does Neolin say?"

Siona was uncomfortable. "Well, that islands are ghost places. That evil people pass over to islands after they die. Old Ayacas—he is a wise man, too, though he is ill now and very old—he does not believe such things. Only, he says that since there is no *need* to go to the island . . . " She stopped short, biting her lip self-consciously. "All right, I *will* go," she said in a rush. Reaching out her hand, she leaped down beside him. "But we haven't a boat and Neolin has. He can be off and away again before we find one."

"Not if we swim. Look, he's going around and down the other side. I can't see him now. Come on!" Dewi pulled the richly embroidered tunic over his head and hung it on a trailing branch. Reaching down, he unhooked the gold cat's collar from Mailcun's neck. Immediately the hound plunged into the water and struck out across the current toward the downstream island. Siona hesitated only a moment, then unfastened her feather cloak and followed Dewi into the morning-blue water in a long, shallow dive.

The island itself was long and narrow, dividing the river into two broad channels. A little less than two hundred yards in length and something more than fifty yards wide, it proved to be a solid outcropping of rock that presented a smooth face above the water line to a height of several feet. Dewi and Siona came to rest standing on the large slippery rocks of a shelf where the water was only waist-deep, and there they caught their breath. Another twenty yards and the current would have swept them past the island's tip and on downstream. Neolin's dugout was nowhere to be seen.

"He's moored it on the other side. He must, if he comes here often." Dewi wiped the water from his face. "You can see this side from your landing place."

The dog Mailcun appeared above them on the bank. He was panting, and giving a good shake, he showered them liberally.

Siona glared up at him and eyed the bank doubtfully. "How are we to get up?"

Dewi shifted his weight, testing the stability of the rock he stood on, and moved from it to another a few feet along the ledge. "Mailcun's gotten up somewhere farther along. But we can manage if we get up to that tree just there. I think I can climb into it."

The tree was a large sycamore squatting on the earth bank above the rock wall, thick-rooted, with long and heavy branches that trailed over the water. Dewi found, however, that pulling himself out of the water was more difficult in the doing than the proposing. He settled for an awkward ascent, pulling a limb down to the water, wrapping his legs around it, and shinnying upward. Once over the ground, he dropped free and, stretching out on the bank, reached down to give Siona a handhold up the slippery rock. A twisted root near the top provided a foothold, and with a wriggle and push she was on the bank. She sat for a moment catching her breath and looking around with great interest.

"It feels so strange! But I suppose it's not, really. It feels very . . . very far away from everywhere, though." She shivered a little and told herself it was because the deep shade was cool and her skin wet.

Dewi called the dog to him. "The man, where is he? Go find him, dog."

Together the boy and girl followed the hound from the built-up bank along the river's edge, down out of the sycamore and sassafras trees into a wild and lovely tangle of wild sweet crabs: thickets of young saplings, mature trees covered with apples-to-be, and the gnarled ruins of their ancestors. *The island of the apple trees. . . .* Dewi and Siona walked through the feathery knee-deep grass and winddrifts of wild flowers, and wondered. How could the oracle—how could anything evil exist in such a place? Perhaps Neolin had gone on to the opposite bank of the river and not to the island at all.

"Look!" Siona caught Dewi's arm. "Oh, look! Was there ever really such a tree?"

A little way beyond, a gigantic tree stump made a dark island in the grass. Much of its outer rim was crumbled away, but the long centuries of the inner rings could still be traced.

"It didn't fall. It was cut down," Dewi said. "Hacked

around with axes and then sawed. But it's been ages ago. Look away there. You can see the long hump under the grass where the trunk and all rotted away."

Siona fingered the rings. "It must have been thousands of years old. Grandfather of all trees."

Dewi raised his head to listen. "I think Mailcun has found something. He's moving back this way. Come."

The dog led them to a point a little above the middle of the island's western rim. There they saw a landing stage and steps cut into the rock. At the foot of the steps Neolin's boat bobbed gently in the water, tied to a heavy copper ring set into the wall beside the bottom stair. A path, not much worn but clearly a path, led from where they stood, south along the rim. They followed it cautiously and had gone perhaps a hundred yards when something caught Dewi's eye. Leaving the path, he strode down into the grass.

"What is it?"

"A bird snare." Kneeling, he cupped his hand gently around the small brown bird so that it could not thrash its wings. "It's not been caught long. The leg seems all right." He plucked the string free and left the frightened bird in the grass to recover itself. He had a worried, puzzled look as he rejoined Siona. "Now why would old greasy-locks want to be snaring birds? It couldn't be anyone else."

Siona was only half listening. "Dewi?" She stopped and pushed her dark, wet hair over her shoulders with a nervous gesture. "This path. Look how the ground is three or four feet higher here along the water than down in the grass among the apple trees. It was the same on the other side, as if it were a mound heaped up a-purpose. It must go all the way around the island."

"Maybe. But there's time enough for that later. Come along."

He ran after Mailcun, who had doubled back impatiently, and Siona hurried behind. As they neared the island's wider downstream end, the rampart where they walked narrowed, tailing off at the last in a series of shallow, rock-cut steps that curved down out of sight around a great rounded hump of rock. This formation thrust up from the river as if the island reared up its head to watch for something on the water. The steps were worn, hollowed in the middle with long use and so weathered that passersby in boats would have taken them for a natural formation.

Dewi gave a soft whistle to summon the dog away from the steps, commanding him to stay quietly on guard, but when he himself crept cautiously down to peer around the outward bulge of the great rock, something—a faint trembling beneath his hand?—made him draw back.

"What is it? Is something wrong?"

Dewi frowned. "I think it's a *cave.* But . . . didn't you feel something just then?"

Siona crept close along the rock. "No. How 'feel'? And how *can* it be a cave? Do you mean the rock is hollow?"

Dewi wondered whether he had imagined the tremor. But he had not imagined the recess in the rock, and the second rock stair. He went first down the sloping stair. At the bottom a walkway two feet above the lapping water led to six high, narrow steps that climbed away from the water to a narrow opening in the weathered rock face. There was no sign of Neolin, but it seemed clear that this place had been his goal. It had a forbidding look, a stark and severe beauty. Time had shaped the stone, giving the effect of slender columns at each side of the portal, and above it a shelf of rock thrust down and outward from the mass to overhang the entrance like a rudely graceful canopy. It effectively hid the opening from the view of anyone not standing close below.

A cautious exploration—the steps were awkwardly steep

—revealed a small domed room beyond the high entrance, but still no sign of Neolin. Stepping into the dim interior, Dewi and Siona found themselves in a cool, dry chamber. It was no cave, but a small round room hollowed from the living rock. And it was uncannily beautiful. They felt almost as if they had stepped outside of time; or was it rather *inside,* at the heart of time? Like the wild tangle of apple trees, like the ancient tree-giant sleeping under the grass, like the island itself, the room had a loveliness and a singing wildness that seemed an echo of some earlier age of fearful beauty and high hearts.

"The island of the apple trees!" Dewi whispered. "Of course! How does it go? *Summer's song is silent,/The island of the apple trees/ Is drowned in war.* The riddle means this place, this island."

Yet what could this place have to do with Aztlán or Cibotlán, or with Neolin, whose wizardry and wisdom were shriveled, spiteful things? This place was all alive, but for the dark shadow of a large niche or alcove off to the right of the entrance. In the room's center a tapering column sprang upward to the ceiling and spread itself in a branching pattern of intricate and formal delicacy: boughs and leaves and singing birds, a leafy canopy carved in stone. The branches dipped low along the walls. Glimpsed through the leaves and around the rim of the floor, water flowed in ripples chiseled on the rock. A stone squirrel ran up the tree's trunk forever, and the tree's stone roots reached out, grew into the floor, and twined there in lacy graven patterns. A wide band marked with strange and graceful signs circled the outer edge of the floor. They were not the letters of Abáloc, but signs shaped with an intricate simplicity that ran and bent and branched as if the words held some singing power Dewi and Siona could sense, but could never hear. As they looked about them, the room moved in their blood, their eyes glowed, and the world beyond the island seemed a shabby place. The wealth and power Cibotlán had wielded were poisonous flowers rooted in the love and fear of death; Abáloc was no more than a dim and pleasant memory; and the men of Gwynet? They had cut the roots that bound them to Gwynet's remembered hills and were adrift, and the edge of the sea receded endlessly before them. . . . All this the children saw and felt in one short moment.

"This room? It *is* the island," Siona whispered, coming awake. She reached out a thin arm, pointing the way they had come. "Out there, too, is the great tree in the center and the water all around. What can it mean?"

As she turned to him, Dewi wondered why he had not noticed how the sheen of her dark hair was like a raven's

wing, how her thin wrist made a fine movement like the water itself when she pointed. And Siona in turn looked at him as if she saw for the first time the keen gray-blue eyes: *hawk's eyes.*

"Oracle or no," he said in a low voice, "it seems an elvish place. The tree's cut down, but the island's still alive. The prophecy said all would come right if the oracle was found. '*Unknown the oracle's round*'? Look you, it *has* to be here somewhere. There is our Serpent—the border around the floor. You said there was a rim around the island. It is here, too. Do you see on the floor how the letters begin just inside the door? The carving on the doorstep is almost too worn to see, but—there and there—you can make it out. The border is like Coala's trinket. It's no circle plain and simple, but a serpent swallowing his own tail."

Suddenly Siona was only a young girl again, thin, wet, and frightened. "But that means—this rock is the head of the island, then. And if Neolin was here, why isn't he now? Please, let's go before we're swallowed! It frightens me. It feels different . . ." Her voice trailed off as a vibration, like the one Dewi had felt outside, trembled softly in the rock's heart. The sun shone brightly on the river, but the dimness in the chamber seemed to deepen.

Dewi told himself firmly that rocks did not swallow. Trust a girl to put it in the most uncomfortable way! But if Neolin had not been swallowed, there was only one place he could have gone. Taking Siona's arm, Dewi pulled her across the room toward the small dark alcove. In its deepest shadow he found a tiny, narrow passage that followed a cleft in the rock, to angle steeply downward. The stair was scarcely eighteen inches wide. Dewi hesitated before going any farther. To turn around on the steps would be next to impossible, and though a dim light guttered far below, the air that pushed up at them like a heavy hand was fetid, foul. As they stood, undecided, a thin, high, moaning chant whispered up to them: Neolin.

"I must go," Dewi insisted, a little wildly, as if it were himself he must convince. He gripped the silver disc where it hung on his breast. "Don't you see? The answer's here. To Diermit's riddle and Coala's oracle and my talisman. It weighs so heavily on me. Nights I dream strange things about it: that I found it in some cave along this river, some cave we passed last night. But that's mad, isn't it? I've not been here before, and there are no cities like the one I dreamed. But if it's true and still to come, I want to *know!*" He plucked at the talisman as if it burned him, and his whisper grew so loud, so insistent, that Siona was terrified Neolin would hear. "Don't you see?" he hissed. "Why are you being so stupid, gaping and hushing at me? The answer to *everything* is down there. Don't you see?"

She shrank from the wild hawk's eyes that glared at her and from the sudden anger that trembled in him, unfolding in his heart like a black and fearful flower. Bewildered, she let go his arm. As he began to grope his way farther into the cleft, she backed away, and only when she found the stone tree at her back, did she realize that she had meant to reach the door . . . to run away . . . to leave the mad boy in this mad place. "I will *not* run," she whispered, crying. Her hands behind her felt the rough, ridged trunk, and in her nervousness she broke off a bit of bark and crumbled it to powder between her thumb and forefinger. *It was alive, not stone.* Her fingers were stained a reddish brown.

"Siona?"

The urgent whisper touched her, and because the tree sang in her blood, she ran into the darkness, fear or no. Dewi had gone no farther than the second step before turning back, but with the narrowness of the place and his own haste, he had wedged foot and knee against the rock and was balanced so precariously on the narrow step that he could not have moved without falling. Siona took his free hand in her two, bracing herself, and he leaned away from her, freeing himself as quietly as he could. In a moment they were safely clear of the passage.

"I couldn't go. It was as if I *had* to, but then he started up again." Dewi shuddered as if shaking himself free of the weight of the darkness. "It was horrible, hearing him. He—he is down there listening only to his own heart. He said things, and there were answers; but it was his own voice answering. He seems to think the Sun Serpent speaks to no one but him, and Coala's trick has made him frantic. So he pleads with himself and taunts himself in a kind of madness."

"But—the oracle? Is it a fable, then?" Siona did not understand. How could so much be true and not that?

"No. *Yes* . . . I don't know!" Dewi leaned his forehead against the tree. "How can it be an oracle if it hasn't any answers? And it hadn't. *But there is something there.* It touched me for a moment. It was like—hating and being afraid of everything. Except me. My inside self. It was hating and being afraid of everything that was not me. There's something horrid down there."

Into the silence that followed, Neolin's faint high chant rose to a pleading note that floated upward into the round room and hung like a deadness in the air. After a while it was loud enough for them to make out the words. He railed and pleaded. "*Lord, will you turn from me for one day's disaster? I have eaten at the heart of Abáloc as my father before me. This morning they were mine—until the troublemakers came, and the strangers with them. But they will be mine again. They will embrace the No which is Your secret name. They will buy life with death as Cibotlán does, and when they do, they shall see how paltry their freedom is beside Your power. Ah, Serpent of the Sun, will you not speak some hope to me? Will you give me no sign, no answer? Do you turn away from my offering?"*

Neolin's heart had no answer to itself. The malignant silence seemed to wait.

"He doesn't understand," whispered Dewi. He had a pale but determined look. "He doesn't understand what he's doing. It takes hold of you and shakes you. . . . We have to help him before something—before he hurts himself."

But the children had taken no more than a step away from the tree when the mad voice broke into a worldless rush of sound like some dumb animal that rages against a pain and bites itself. Dewi and Siona struggled toward the stair, but the darkness and a beating hatred pressed against them.

"Then . . . then I say NO to thee as well!"

The cry throbbed in the heavy air. Stone rang against stone, and with the crash that followed, the rock itself trembled, and the chamber darkened as if night had fallen over the river in the summer's midafternoon. The island stirred and shuddered, and the children clung to each other and the tree. A black wind rose in the darkness, and the tree groaned and creaked in that wind, and the water rushed around the walls. Branches flailed, and the roots strained beneath their feet, but it seemed as if the tree sang, and the birds in it.

Then, at last, it was over. The shimmering, tossing leaves and water were once more only lines chiseled in stone and the tree trunk a patterned, branching column. The darkness was gone from the alcove, and the only sound was a loud lapping of water at the steps outside. Dewi and Siona ran to the entrance.

The lowest step was awash. They stood above it and saw

the water rippling outward, a V shape moving south away down the river from the island, spreading out toward the river's banks in a wide, frothing wake. Afterward the children said they could not be sure, because of the way the afternoon sun gleamed on the river, but as they stood watching, it seemed some gigantic ghost-shape cleaved the water. A dark shadow on the water, longer than the island, swimming as a snake swims . . .

4

Summer's Song

Moments after Dewi, Siona, and the dog Mailcun had returned to the village of Abáloc in Neolin's dugout, the brothers Amalahtis and Lincoas took men with them to the island, and there they buried their wise man, a man so jealous of his wisdom and ambitious of power that he lost hold of the one and, to gain the other, opened his heart to darkness. He was found in the rock-cut lower chamber with an ancient long-handled bronze hammer lying beside his hand. Around him on the floor were the fragments of the carved stone serpent he had shattered, clubbing it down from the sloping ceiling. Pieces of the ceiling had fallen with it. Neolin had, after all, died at his own hand.

The chamber itself was a great wonder to the young king and prince of Abáloc. On the undamaged portion of the ceiling there remained a niche carved to represent a cleft in the rock wall, and from it two young pumas, carved in high relief, leaped toward the narrow stair. The serpent itself had been represented as moving toward the cleft and, through it, to the roots of the island. Seeing this and the upper chamber, the young men were bewildered, and they found other things that made them marvel: books written in the old tongue of Abáloc, so long lost to them and still so difficult to read; intricately chased goblets of a metal something like silver; ancient garments so rotten with the damp that only their heavy embroideries of gold thread and pearls survived; curious boxes made of rose quartz set in gold and holding polished stones the colors of wine and moon and water.

They took nothing away. "Ayacas must see it first," they said. "What a city the Citadel of the Moon must have been!" they marveled. "For these things can only have come to Neolin from his grandfather, who was the grandson of the wise man who led Abáloc down from that place. Now that we have the books and the maps, only think: we will see it for ourselves!"

Old Ayacas, when he came several days later, agreed that Neolin's forefathers must have known the island even in the days before the Northern Wars. Supported by Erilla's sons, Ayacas stood at the foot of the stair that led up into the rock and shook his head wonderingly. "Since I was a boy, I have dreamed of this place," he said. "From the beginning when I was apprenticed to the wise man Olin, I knew that he came here. But he passed the deeper lore and the secrets of the wise only to Neolin, though I was the elder, and I was forbidden to come here. It is good to have done with such prohibitions, for they are breeders of darkness. But come, I must see these marvels!"

The others helped his slow progress, for he had been ill of the fever and was still not well. However, like the others in Abáloc whom it had touched, and like the Companions, he had that resistance to its virulence that the tribes of Cibotlán did not have. Coala's "prophecy," based upon her sharp observation and her memory of an earlier pestilence, had been true before she spoke it. The seven cities would be years in recovering—if their old enemies to the south and west did not come like wolves and ravens to finish them. Scouts sent south along the river from Abáloc reported a great wailing, and towering fires in the city of Tucrikán, where infected houses were being burned. Half the city lay waste. The people of Abáloc, freed from a long and oppressing danger, and from the need to flee, had unpacked their waiting boats and turned to nursing their own sick.

When Ayacas had gone into the rock, Queen Erilla, Madauc and Dewi, Coala, Siona, and those who had come with them in the boats climbed the stair around the rock's side and came onto the island of the apple trees. From the head of the stair they saw the tree-clad rampart branching east and west, curving out from the great rock and lost in a moment among the sycamores that screened the fields of apple trees from the village's view. In several places close to the rock (and as they later found, at many points on the island's rim) the earth was humped and cracked. In some spots the earthen rampart had fallen into the river, carrying with it a few young and less firmly rooted trees.

Madauc was in a strange, restless mood. The elation that followed on the success of their dangerous and exhilarating masquerade had died away. That trick had served them well, for undoubtedly it had saved lives; but there had been little other reward, for the golden horde had left little of any value in the trampled fields. When he thought of the riches that the fleeing army had stripped from the fever-stricken soldiers who had already fallen, Madauc wavered between regret and self-reproach: regret for the lost plunder, and disgust that he should regret it. Were the Companions of the Western Sea not something better than carrion crows after all?

To Erilla he said, "Now that your oracle is found and

seems no longer to have a tongue, perhaps your people will be singing their summer songs at last, as the old prophecy has it. Yet I could wish we had been something more than lookers-on. It will be a heavy winter that has no songs of battle and high deeds, no bragging tales to lighten it."

"Only lookers-on? You were more than that," the lady Erilla demurred. A fall of sunlight gave her rich brown hair a sheen of gold. Fine crinkles spread under her eyes as she smiled and looked up at him curiously. "Does it irk you so to see a war won without battle? Are all the men of Gwynet such barbarians?"

He started and looked uncomfortable. "But that is unfair, my lady!" Honestly distressed, he asked, "Have we seemed so to you, then?"

She returned his look with an innocent air of challenge. "I am sure I do not know. But I think you did not come across the wide sea of ocean in answer to an ancient verse about an oracle that oppressed an unnamed, unknown land."

He laughed ruefully, but whether from amusement or self-mockery it was difficult to tell. "A hit! Oh, I suppose when I was a boy, that seemed reason and more to set out adventuring. But you are right. I fear I must admit that when I grew to be a man, I remembered the other part of the tale: the woman in that long-ago shipwreck and her dress of pearls."

Erilla smiled. Coala, who had been listening intently, snatching at the meaning of words and phrases she had learned, looked up sharply. Dewi noticed and wondered whether she still worried about the "golt" she had promised them in Abáloc—where men wore golden hats and ate off golden plates. He was not sure if Madauc still held all that against her. One or two of the men did, and their grumbling had soured a little these past few summer days, otherwise pleasantly enough spent in salting fish and baking hard corn cakes for the homeward voyage and in stitching new boots and fur cloaks.

"And so you go home empty-handed." Erilla's observation was matter of fact. "But what of the boy? He looks uneasy to hear you speak so. Why did you wish to come so far, Dewi?"

Dewi flushed, and some of the Companions laughed. Mad Dewi's dreams, they thought. But it was not so simple a thing as a dream. How could he explain what he scarcely understood? The answer came—where from, he was never sure—in a rush of words. "I think because . . . because I wished I could someday live in the wild, and follow a prince's banner, and . . . and come to an island like this, and sail down the Great River to the sea!"

Erilla smiled. "One, at least, does not return home quite empty-hearted." Turning to Madauc, she asked, "When do you think to go?"

He stood on the high bank and watched the water pass. "In a day or two," he said. "The sooner the better. We must finish making new ropes for *Gwennan Gorn*, our ship, in case the damp has rotted those we left with her. We had a new sail ready-made and wrapped in waxed cloth, so there's no worry there. Yes, if we mean to be home before November and her storms, we must go soon. A day or two." There was an odd, strained note to the words. Madauc made a quick gesture of impatience, as if he were angry with himself or at some thing he could not put a name to.

There was an unhappy silence, and then a rush of conversation as everyone tried to fill it up at once. Coala appeared suddenly at Siona's side to whisper, unheard by the others, "Please, explain me. Why do they speak of this boat?"

The explanation deepened the shadow in her dark eyes.

The blue flower on her cheek was bright and unnatural against the pale, delicate skin. "I see," she said.

Siona turned to dart a questioning look at Dewi and did not see the older girl turn away. But Dewi watched her move down through the grass and into the tangled apple trees. He shrugged. There was no reading that odd little flower face.

"Here is Ayacas." Erilla hurried to meet the old counselor. "What do you make of these chambers, old friend?"

The old man had been much moved. "Clearly, my queen, this has been an ancient place of power. And just as clearly, it is no longer so. The upper room has a simple and matchless beauty, but, my apologies to our two young friends, the tree and songbirds *are* no more than stone, and I felt no evil in the deeper place. What power it was that the place had, in another age, we cannot know. Yet it is curious . . ."

Siona shyly slipped her hand into Dewi's, and secretly he was glad of it. The ugly horror of the darkness in that deep room had been true enough, and he did not like to think what might have happened had he been alone. He would have lost himself more utterly than—than when? Perhaps only people were the real talismans. Perhaps . . .

". . . curious about these talismans," Ayacas was saying. "Much of whatever truth the upper room holds in its symbols of tree and serpent and the rest is lost to us. The first of the *Books of the Kings of Abáloc* and the books found in the lower chamber may tell us something, but I would hazard that even in the days of the Northern Wars with Aztlán, there was confusion whether the Serpent was snake or circle; whether the figure was tree or winged man or bird. All of us—Abáloc, Cibotlán, these young men from beyond the sea—have read the shapes, each in his own way. But do you not see? In one sense we have all touched the truth at some point. The inner figure of the symbol must in some way mean life or freedom: fruitfulness, and all that we can stretch ourselves to. The ring? It is for each a sign of containment, of 'time' perhaps. I am not sure. But as the prophecy our friends tell us of has said, the balance of these things had been destroyed. For both Aztlán and Cibotlán the Serpent meant time only in his guise as Death: a dark god indeed."

"What other guise has time, then, old man?" Madauc turned suddenly from his morose contemplation of the river. "It is a great killer of hopes, I think."

"Why, we can act nowhere but within time," said the old man, reaching out a hand in helpless compassion. "Only a fool would deny its power, yet only a fool would make it his god! We must hope that the balance is restored to this land. In the old figures below, the serpent who swallows his own tail seems not only a ring that encloses life, but also an emblem of endlessness, of eternity, if you will. Does it not seem so to you? An act made within time is an act made in eternity, for surely it can never be undone, though it may perhaps be repaired. Yes, death does end us all—my own time is not far off. But once you have looked on time's power with clear eyes, my friend, you are freed to grow and to create. Surely that is what the tree means. Or, if you prefer, as young Dewi's talisman has it, you are free to spread your wings."

"It seems a strange freedom that begins in being bound," said Madauc, unconvinced. Then he was sorry, for he saw the depth of the old man's concern. "I am sorry. It is a lesson I have had read to me before, and it may be no fault but my own that it has a hollow sound. I am glad that all comes right now for your people after so long a time. But what I find at home when we come there is more like to be outlawry than honor. I hope that what you will find in your *Dunom o'r Plagro tan'e Menet*, your City of the

Moon under the Mountain, may bring you home at last."

"It is my great wish to see it," Ayacas said simply.

Erilla, divining a little of what troubled the tall young man, said thoughtfully, "But we do not, *must* not, think of it as our lost paradise, to be gained again and held forever fast. We must not tie our hearts to the past now that we begin to rediscover it. To do so is to listen to the dark voice within us, for *we* are different from our forebears who lived in the city. We shall see. If it is still safe, perhaps we will return here. Abáloc is where *we* are."

Amalahtis nodded. "I have thought, too, and my brother with me, of how much wide, rich country stands empty in the deserted lands."

It was a new idea to many and stirred much excited talk. But through it all, Dewi's thoughts echoed with Madauc's words: *"I hope what you will find . . . may bring you home at last."* In that darkness where Neolin wrestled with his own dark voice, Dewi had for one terrifying moment remembered and struggled to be that other self, to break through time and regain the safety of a life marked off with rules and clocks and bells. But to try to be someone you were not—what was that but a way of dying? His heart was not in that other place because he could—no, because he *had* never been himself there. And Gwynet? Gwynet was little more than a remembered confusion of hardship, color and excitement, brutality and chance beauties. This place, Abáloc? No, not the place; but the life. It seemed clear at last. Home was not a "here". It was the quiet feeling itself, the end to running.

"Couldn't I stay? Not go?" He dropped the question, with an inflexion of surprise, into the middle of a conversation, where it floated down like a feather in the sudden, listening silence.

Red Kynon, who had been sitting quietly with his back against the great rock, put in uneasily, as if he knew it was not the best of times for the news, "Some five or six of the men are saying the same, Captain. It seems they would marry and be setting themselves up as fishermen."

Madauc looked at him blankly. Then, mastering his surprise, he managed a bleak smile. "It's that way, is it? Well enough, then. But *Gwennan Gorn* cannot spare more than six hands. If any others are of the same mind, they will have to choose lots and settle it among themselves." He did not even look at Dewi, but turned abruptly and walked away.

Dewi was miserable. A flat refusal would have been less bewildering. At the beginning there had been a companionship between Madauc and himself much closer and freer than that of master and boy, but it had grown no deeper. In fact, it had seemed to grow less. Why should Madauc be angry, then? Dewi wavered, unsure whether he should follow and ask again whether he might be one of the six to stay.

Ayacas rested a hand on his shoulder, both to restrain and reassure him. "It is never easy to find the way that is your own and not what another dreams for you. Your prince must stumble upon his own road, for I think he never will be shown it. But you, Dewi? We shall be glad of your staying, if indeed you do. Lincoas tells me you have some little scholarship. We will be glad of that, too."

Lincoas smiled. "Who is to say? Perhaps one day you will be the one to unravel the riddle of our ancient kinship."

Dewi only half attended to their kindness, for he was still looking unhappily after the prince as he disappeared among the trees.

"The young *fool!*" Prince Madauc slashed at the wild flowers powdered through the grass with a crooked switch broken from a crab apple tree.

"Something is bad?"

Coala sat, small and straight-backed, on the ruin of the great tree stump, her feet invisible in the grass, as if she grew there.

"Something bad? Oh, there you are." Madauc frowned, scarcely seeing her. "Bad? The boy wishes to stay. First Ithil is sent to his death, then Llywarch goes his own way, and now Ithil's son. Blood brothers, sworn brothers, it all comes to nothing. But what use is there in telling you, little one? You cannot understand." He stood glowering down at her, seeing only Ywein and all the loved and familiar faces that seemed to have looked at and through and past him and gone on.

"Can I not?" There was a faint tartness in the reply.

A little startled, Madauc woke out of himself.

Coala looked up at him. "I work hard to learn. The young girls and boys, they teach me. Never late for learning, they say."

He smiled. "You make it sound as if you were an old woman, child."

"I have seen many bad things," she said simply. "My heart had sixteen years' happiness, then no more mother-father. Two years now are bad. It was for Tochtlú I run away, you know? But it is for me, too, now. I stop." She regarded him thoughtfully. "But you have no stopping place. Is it not so? You fear you float always down the river, like a leaf, never come again to shore. That cannot be right."

He sat himself down in the tall grass and, leaning against the stump, plucked blades of grass and began to braid them into a ring. "No?" he said.

"No." She nodded in a very decided fashion. "Are you a leaf? No, you are not. If you do not like downriver, you go upriver, or other river all-to-gether. Where you find a touching-down place for your heart, you feel both at once most safe and free. And real. Not perhaps happy," she added wistfully. "But real."

Madauc tried to laugh at her solemnity, but he could not. The hermit Gruffyt and his peace, Ayacas and his paradoxes—neither had touched him so. Perhaps they were the same in the end, but neither explained his longing nor moved him so deeply as this slender girl who twisted her fingers in her lap and spoke of "a touching-down place for your heart."

"It may be," he said. And then after a moment he reached for what seemed far safer ground. "But the boy is a fool. He *can* go home to Gwynet, to study at Bangor as was planned for him. He is quiet, is Dewi, and sometimes a bit strange, but he is sharp. He might be a great man one day, and yet he wishes to throw all that away."

Coala gave an impatient shrug and pushed her long black hair over her shoulders. "You say it only because you are *not* a great man in that place. Is it so much more good than this place, then? I think it sounds—how do you say? —*barbaric*." The dusky cheek under the blue flower was flushed.

"So it may be," he answered slowly. "But there are many good hearts there, and could they live in peace it would be the best of lands."

"It was wrong of me to name it so," Coala said miserably. "It is only that I sorrow you must go away. I will be very alone."

"Will you?" He looked at her searchingly. "But these folk will be good to you. And you have Tochtlú."

"Yes."

Madauc stirred. "We must go. They will be waiting for us at the boats."

"Yes. I come," Coala said. Then, hesitantly, her dark eyes meeting his blue ones, she whispered, "Please? It is so glad you are not the god."

Neither of them could recall afterward quite how it had happened. Madauc, before he fully knew what he did in that tearing, unfolding, flowering moment, pulled her down to him and kissed her. He held her so for one slow and wondering moment. In the next he had disappeared through the tangle of the orchard , and Coala found herself sitting alone in the grass with her amazement. When the boats were ready to leave, Dewi and Siona came looking and found her lost in some thought, her hands still folded in her lap. She smiled and then, with a sudden doelike shyness, was gone.

Dewi shrugged. "If she doesn't come quickly, she'll be having to swim back, then." He turned again toward the landing place and missed seeing the curious, speculative look in Siona's eyes. She laughed quietly to herself and hurried behind.

No one of them saw the straight green shoot that pushed up through the grass where it lapped at the foot of the great tree felled long years before, in the days that shaped the Northern Wars. It was left to grow unseen.

Three days later the coracles went into the river with the dawn: dark cockleshells heavily laden, riding as deep as that morning of midsummer when they had come, carrying almost twice the number. All of the folk of Abáloc were gathered among the sycamores beside the quay to watch, but for all of the bright garments, and the playing of musicians, it was a somber greeting to a shining August day. Arthfael and Merfyn and the others who stayed behind brought the last baskets to be stowed in the coracles and handed them from the edge of the stone pier to the men in the boats. Several were still to be loaded when Madauc noticed that their lids were tied with red cord, strangely knotted.

"What are these? These are not ours." He made a sign that they should be taken away.

The young king Amalahtis held up a hand to counter the command. "No, Prince of Gwynet. They are yours indeed, the gift of us all. If they may not help you to your heart's desire, still they may buy land for your men and some comfort for yourself."

Lincoas smiled a little mockingly, as a man may to a friend. "We would not have you go sailing empty-handed home from the lands of legend. Who would believe you had not summered in some nearer southern haven?" He knelt to untie the cords.

The baskets brimmed with pearls, all the treasure they had worn to face the armies of Cibotlán, and more. They were freshwater pearls and small, but perfect; and many were unstrung, sorted according to color and size and tied up in little cotton sacks. The famous pearl mussels of Conwy River in Gwynet did not yield a finer harvest. The Companions were speechless at the slight.

"It is a gift indeed," said Madauc at last. "And I fear I have a poor grace for accepting gifts, for which you must forgive me. It comes of so long having to fight for every gain. But such thanks as I have are yours." He watched as the baskets were fastened up again and loaded, and then said, "What you say is true, I know. They will call us liars if they can. Yet I begin to wonder if that is the defeat I would have thought it even three days ago. There are many good farms and boats in such a treasure as this. And if there proves to be no place for me in Gwynet, perhaps I will go to my brother Rhirid in Ireland. What then, I cannot say."

It was as if he struggled to put into words uncertainties that words can scarcely carry. His eyes searched out Coala where she stood beside Queen Erilla, and it seemed to some that it was to her he spoke rather than to Dewi and the six who stayed behind. "I make no promises. I cannot. But if *Gwennan Gorn* found a willing crew, I would return one day. I *cannot* promise. But . . . it seems it is what I wish."

Then he stepped into the coracle, and the oarsmen pushed out into the stream. It moved into the current, pulling out into the wide river and away.

"*Come back!*" Dewi almost cried out aloud, and then looked around uneasily, half thinking he must have done so. Nor was he sure that he did not imagine the answer that drifted back to Abáloc, a whisper on the water.

"I *will* come!"

5
Full Circle

The boy called David Reese crouched in the wet coolness of the culvert under the highway and listened. No one had missed him yet. Before long, Aunt Milly would be calling, "*Da*-vee! *Lu*-unch!" in a voice like a trumpet, and ringing the bell outside the farmhouse kitchen door. He would be too far away by then to hear. He stooped to untie his tennis shoes, took them off, thrust his socks into a jeans pocket, and knotted the shoestrings carefully together. Then he stepped out into the shallow stream. The sand and pebbles felt good under his toes. Hunched over, he splashed along under the highway and came out in a tree-shaded cut that climbed easily down to the river, a wooded water-stair that cut the cornfields atop the bluffs in two. He did not want any lunch. He did want desperately to think, to work things out. Aunt Milly's cheerfulness, Uncle Jim's guided tour of the new milking room, and worst of all, the arrival of cousin Charles with his talkative wife, Noonie, and Alice, their little girl—they had made the big farmhouse ring with laughter. It had almost smothered him, so he had fled.

Dave had not wanted to come up to the farm at all. There was too much to do at home; still was. If he could manage to finish the problems in the second-year physics textbook he had checked out of the school library as summer reading, and if he could spend just a little more time on the Suetonius and Pliny Mr. Trumbull was so fond of, he would have a much better chance in the advanced placement exams Fettles Academy gave during the last week in August. If he could skip an entire year in both subjects, and do the same with modern European history and English lit next year, and one more subject the year after . . . he could go to the university while he was still sixteen!

But Mr. Reese had been adamant; angry, in fact. "*I* need a vacation, and Mrs. Bellick needs a vacation from *you*. It will probably take her the better part of the week to clean up that mess of ink spots and paper scraps and chemical stinks you call a bedroom. Good Lord, Dave! We haven't been up to the farm since Christmas, and your Uncle Jim will be hurt if you turn him down again. And for what? The *Lives of the Caesars*? When I was a kid, you couldn't have *paid* me to read Pliny in August. Oh, Suetonius, is it? Well, you couldn't have paid me to read him in August either. Dammit, if you didn't look so disgustingly healthy, I'd send you over to Doc Norman at the clinic for a checkup. It's unnatural, that's what it is!"

He had ordered Dave to finish packing and slammed back into his study, still grumbling. Dave, determined but dutiful, packed with meticulous care: shirts and underwear in plastic bags; for emergencies, extra shoelaces, a box of chocolate-covered graham crackers, Kleenex, and the battered Boy Scout first-aid kit; and on top, *Adventures in Physics* and *De Vita Caesarum.*

Dave held onto a scrubby tree that grew beside the falling stream and stretched to gain a safe foothold below. It was rotten luck that he had neither book with him now. If he had some work to do, he wouldn't feel so adrift, so apprehensive. His father and Mrs. Bellick had managed it very neatly, and they had meant well, but it had ruined the day—the week, probably. This morning's last-minute addition to his suitcase of a freshly ironed handkerchief for his Sunday suit must have provided the occasion for the last-minute abstraction of the two schoolbooks. After the two-hour drive, unpacking in the sunny old-fashioned loft bedroom of the old Reese homestead an hour ago, Dave had been sick when he found them gone: cold and trembling, and his stomach as hard and tight as a baseball. It frightened him because he could not think, could not remember, why it was so important. There had been a reason. There must have been. Learning mattered horribly. The more you had in your head, the safer you were, the less you had to worry. But he could not answer "Safer from what?" or why he should worry. The work itself was the only worry he could put a name to. Yet, always, he felt this pushing hurry and the craving for security.

He had come to the river. The memory of it was dim, a little confused, but a few minutes' aimless searching found the hidden ancient path through the trees that grew on the steep, sloping bank below the bluffs, and cautiously he made his way along it. In places it was crumbled away, and here and there a sycamore tree had rooted and grown on the path itself and had to be climbed around. Dave almost missed seeing the first cave for the tangle of vines that hung over its shallow recess. Where the second cave opened into the climbing hill, the path widened to a broad shelf and made a sort of sun trap at midday. He remembered the place only dimly, more as if he had been told about it than seen it. *But I have been here. I have.* He held onto the thought doggedly. He had found a medallion here last autumn. The silver disc he had lost so soon after. That was when the dreams had begun to get better. They had been strange, fearful dreams about hunger, about a harsh, bearded master who beat him, and of having to sleep with beasts and eat scraps as if he had not been a free man's son. But the dreams had become less and less real. Only . . . *only better not think about them.*

He pushed under the creepers and into the cave. It was cool and dry, being well above the water, and the floor was sandy. Squatting down, he sifted sand between his fingers. There might still be arrowheads. The thing to do would be to make a sifting box with a piece of window screen and shovel all of the sand through it. Finding a sharp-edged piece of stone near the back wall, he bent to peer at it in the dim light from the cave opening.

A sound outside startled him. A squirrel? A pebble rattling down the slope? It made him jump a little, and the glasses, which he kept forgetting to push up when they slipped down the bridge of his nose, fell off. The world shrank to a pale blur of light that was the cave's entrance, and he groped frantically along the wall. He had already lost two pair since last autumn. He couldn't lose these, too. Crawling forward a foot or two, he ran his hands lightly over the floor. At the same moment his left hand touched the eyeglasses, his right hand, which had moved along the wall, brushed against empty space. Dave fumbled the glasses on. The darkness at the back of the cave was too deep for seeing, but his hands found the place where the wall stopped. The passage was low, just large enough to crawl through, but the room beyond was large enough for Dave to stand upright. He felt an unaccustomed excitement, almost anticipation. Oddly, he did not mind the pitch darkness. Groping, he measured the chamber in his mind's eye. He must come back tomorrow; bring a flashlight. Since he didn't have any schoolwork with him, it wouldn't really be wasting time. Still, as if to reassure himself, he decided that if he found anything interesting, he might work it up into an essay: *"Some Flint Points and Hand Axes of Belmont County," by D. A. Reese.*

He found the jar only by falling over it. It rolled a little way, making a hollow, rumbling sound, easy to follow. An excitement for once too strong to drown in caution and the fear of disappointment made his hands shake as he ran them over the oblong cylinder. It had a knob at one end: a tall jar with the knobbed lid sealed. It would not come free. In awkward haste Dave blundered his way to the passage, pushed the jar through, and wriggled after it.

Scrambling to his feet and hurrying forward, Dave stumbled in his eagerness and shattered the pottery jar on the flat rock shelf outside the cave's mouth. The gasp that escaped him was half for a badly scraped knee and half for surprise. A thick roll of parchment lay among the shards and slivers. Arrowheads, beads, even pearls would have been less a puzzle; certainly less of a disappointment. With a sigh for the lost jar, he smoothed out the curled leaves with a shaky hand. The writing was cramped, crowded onto the pages, strangely familiar. Bewildered, he traced his finger along the first line and began wonderingly to decipher the spidery Latin script. It began, "*Prope dedidici* . . ."

I have forgot almost how to hold a pen. It is a strange thing to see my knuckles sharp bent and my nails white with pushing a scratching point across a sheet of vellum. The pen is of my own making—a goose quill trimmed with the knife my lord gave me that had been his dead brother's, the lord Rien's. The ink we brewed from oak galls, and I hope it will not fade. Red Kynon remembers from his youth that the monks used oak galls, but whether they steeped them in vinegar or boiled them, he did not recall. So for good measure I have done both.

Strangest of all is to think that this vellum is all that's left of the last of our sheep. Red Kynon has a proper curve-bladed knife and some knowledge of many useful crafts, and so we saved and dressed all of the skins. If I am careful to waste no space with margins and to keep my pen well trimmed and my characters small, our tale may just be told before I come to the tail end of the poor little flock descended from the only ewe and ram to survive that long second voyage, with Madauc and

Rhirid in *Gwennan Gorn* and the *Pedr Sant.* I am sorry to think they are all gone, for though the fine deer of this land are plentiful and tasty, and though sheep are stupid and contrary enough to drive any sheep dog wild in this woodland country, there are few things sweeter to the tooth than young lamb roasted with herbs and well basted. But the old ram killed himself with falling off a cliff, so that the two young ones need must fight to see which should rule the flock, and the wolves came, drawn by the smell of blood, and ate the both of them. Madauc only laughed and said rams and wolves together put him in mind of the old days in Gwynet, his half brothers all tearing at each other's throats as soon as old Ywein their father was buried in Bangor churchyard. Well, with naught left but ewes, we ate mutton until we were sick of it, for there would be no lambing time for us next year or ever, and it was as well to make an end of them. We will be moving again come apple time, and no sheep to slow us down. What will the dogs do, I wonder? They will be lost with no slow heels to nip at and strays to manage. One day their pups may make passable hunters. But the old dogs ? . . . I know what it is to be lost.

Indeed, I cannot untangle the whole of myself, let alone the whole history of our coming from Gwynet to this place, and the marvels of the City of the Moon under the Mountain. That was a splendid place! But we did not stay there long, for we felt dwarfed in its great, cold halls and missed the open hillsides. The account of it belongs more with the tales in the old *Books of the Kings.*

My lords Madauc or Rhirid or even Red Kynon could give better account of their part of this tale, but Madauc and Rhirid have more important matters to employ them—dismantling the iron furnace and the old fish weirs and seeing the fortifications of the new hill town well begun before we move from this place we have outgrown—and Red Kynon protests that he swore off writing when he left off studying to be a priest. I have done much reading in the old histories of the kings of Abáloc, but I fear my skill in Latin is rusted from long disuse. There is almost enjoyment in trying it again. They say that Father Gwillim taught me my grammar and calligraphy, and that when I was a boy, I wished to be a monk so that I could always be reading and copying at books. I do not really remember. Or rather, I remember more surely other things, which they laugh at and call "mad Dewi's dreams." Mad Dewi. I am a man now, and tall and broad enough to laugh at any who use that old name in jest. But even so, sometimes it touches me. Mad Dewi. I wonder, did people in that other place call the other boy such names?

No. It is no good to toy with such tormenting thoughts. I would not change this place of his for my old one for all the gold in Gwynet or all the pearls in the river. Our sons and daughters grow tall here, and free. From where I sit in the house above the waterfall, I see them climbing among the rocks and daring the water, brown-skinned elves, and the littlest like hobmen, round and quick. Some are fair-haired and others reddish or dark brown, but all of them have the gray-blue eyes. The black-haired one is young Rien, Madauc's son. And Red Kynon, for all of his mistrust of women, brought a young wife from Ireland, so we are well supplied with small "fire bushes" as Siona calls them. Our own small daughter, sharp-tongued Elen of the straight brown hair, stands stranded on a rock where the water froths whitest, but the falls drown her furious screaming, and the boys squat on the wet rocks above and laugh. They know her. If she were truly frightened, she would not scream.

No, all in all, I would change nothing that has happened—not even the need that turns me scholar-historian at this late day. Some say I undertake a pointless labor, for who is there to read our chronicle? But I shall translate it into the tongue of Abáloc for our children and leave this copy in a place I know of."

On the following sheet the story unfolded itself: *Here begins the History of Davyt Rhys known as Dewi ap Ithil, and of the Strife in Gwynet which brought Madauc, a Prince of that Land, Twice over the Sea's Edge; and of how Abáloc was left to the Descendants of the Northmen, and of our Wanderings since that Time.*

Davyt Rhys . . . David Reese . . .

Dave read hungrily, stumbling over unfamiliar names, torn between fascination and alarm. Here and there the ancient manuscript was stained and illegible, but he read quickly, taking the gist of what he could not clearly decipher or understand. It was like walking into a remembered dream. Castle Dolwydlan, Razo, Father Gwillim—they were as vivid as if he had seen them himself. As if. . . . And then he knew that it had been no dream. But after Dolwydlan the tale was all strange, the faces shadowed. Time forgotten, he read feverishly. How he wished he had seen Tushcloshán from the Hills, Tucrikán from the river, the golden horde of Cibotlán on the fields and hills beyond Abáloc! He might have *been* the one to see them if only he had not longed so to be safe and away. And then again, he might not. No, *he* would have gone to Bangor instead. He would have shut himself safe away from chance and choice. He did not quite understand why it should be so, but it seemed that with that recognition he shed the worry that weighed him down as if it were an old garment, a winter skin.

The sun was gone from the riverbank, and the shadow of the bluffs crept across the water. The wooded hills on the other side of the river gleamed green and golden in the summer afternoon before he came to the last sheets, which were too much damaged to be read. As he turned them over carefully—for they were dry and cracked—a blackened disc slid from between them, dropped, and rolled along the worn, uneven path.

A small foot slapped down on it just as it wobbled to the river side.

"What'll you give me for it?" said Alice. She held out the tarnished medallion.

Dave took it and weighed it in his hand. Perhaps for a little while it had possessed a power beyond the common virtue of things, but now it was only a curious ornament of blackened silver. "You can have it for nothing," he said, returning it to his small cousin. "Dad'll be glad it's found, but I don't need it any more, I guess. It's real silver. No, really it is. It'll be pretty when it's polished up. I don't need it any more," he repeated.

"Thank you," said Alice with seven-year-old solemnity. She produced a grubby handkerchief, wrapped the ringed figure carefully, and put it away in the deepest pocket of her jeans. "What's that?" She pointed to the roll of browned and crackling pages.

"It's a story. About—about somebody I used to know."

"Oh. *I* can read," said Alice, and then, "It looks awfully dirty. Why didn't you come to lunch? We had hamburgers on the barbecue, and apple pie after. Were you just being difficult?"

Dave grinned. "Who said that? My dad?"

"No, I just thought you might be." She sat down cross-legged and watched him as if she were undecided whether she approved of him or not. "I'm being difficult, too," she said after a moment. "Some people came to visit after lunch, but there weren't any little kids, and I don't like to sit and listen, so I hid and then ran away. I didn't know you'd be here. You wouldn't like to go back and see who's come to visit, would you?" she asked hopefully.

"Are you trying to get rid of me, Alice?" He pushed his glasses up his nose and looked at her sternly, in a very good imitation of his father.

Alice sighed. "Well, then. I don't suppose you'd want to come on an adventure?" She pulled at her lip and eyed him doubtfully. "I've been planning it for weeks. If you don't mind rowing, you're welcome to come. I *was* a little bit worried about the rowing."

"I think—" Dave said, matching her solemnity, "I think it's just the day for going on an adventure. What exactly did you have in mind?" He wondered if he were a little light-headed from going without lunch. But there seemed to be nothing but this moment, and this funny, skinny little cousin, brown-skinned and blue-eyed, already hurrying upstream along a thread of path he had never noticed. Dave scrambled to his feet, looked around for a small rock to place on top of the leaves of old manuscript to weight them down, and ran after her.

Alice led him through a tangle of underbrush and a swampy patch of black gum trees to a small nook of a beach. There, on the shady slope above the little mud flat, he saw a small overturned rowboat, propped up all around with stones and sticks and glistening a bright, ugly green. Dave recognized the color. It was the one Aunt Milly used on anything and everything to be painted ("A good outdoor color," she called it). The rocks and earth around the boat were generously decorated with the same unnatural hue.

"I didn't have a very good brush," Alice explained, testing the paint with a finger. "It cost twenty-five cents, but the hairs kept coming out."

The boat was a runaway. Sometime during the winter it had come to rest in this sheltered place, and Alice had found it one day during Easter vacation. She had come to visit it every weekend her family had spent at the farm until, in June, when still no one had come and fetched it away, she spent a whole morning getting it out of the water, washing out the leaves and dirt, and wrestling it over on its back. She had kept it a secret, and last Saturday she had painted it.

"You should've scraped and sanded it first," Dave said, eying the lumpy finish critically.

"I didn't know." She looked at it anxiously.

"We could always do it later," he added hastily. "I suppose it's not a bad job, all things considered. Let's see if it floats." He was thinking that it was a good thing he had come along. He had an uncomfortable conviction that Alice would have been well on her way to Cincinnati before she discovered how much of an adventure she had undertaken.

" 'She,' " corrected Alice. "Boats are shes."

Dave made an uncomplimentary snorting sound as he righted the little boat and shoved it into the water. A length of fresh clothesline had been attached to the staple in the prow, and this he tied to a stout root growing out of the bank. Then he stepped into the little green boat and jiggled his weight back and forth.

"No bad leaks, anyway. It—*she* didn't happen to have any oars, did she?"

Alice dragged them down from where she had propped them across two low branches for painting. Her small thin face shone with delight. "We're really going? And you aren't going to tell? Where are we going?"

Dave began to have misgivings as he laid the stubby oars along the thwarts. "I suppose Aunt Milly—I suppose your grandma will want us soon, so we can clean up for dinner. But, well, maybe we could go a little way upstream just to see how she handles." He stepped forward into the bow and jumped easily onto the bank.

If Alice was disappointed at the prospect of such an unimaginative expedition, she was still very quick in scrambling aboard and settling herself down in the stern. Dave untied the painter and clambered in, rocking the boat so alarmingly in the process that Alice sobered even further.

"Um, Davy? Can you swim?" Her forehead was puckered in a frown.

"Sure." He pulled sharply with his left-hand oar, watching over his shoulder until they had come around so that the bow pointed out of the little cove. He laughed. "How come? Were you thinking you might have to save me if we sink?"

Alice giggled and folded her hands on her knees, and grew still with delight.

Then they were on the river. The water was murky, there were swirls of detergent suds, a bottle, an occasional dead fish, and a faint, unpleasant smell of sewage. Yet despite all that, the world was only the river and the green, green hills. Far upstream the water shimmered in the summer haze as if it flowed from the summer sky itself, and a long, wooded island hung in the golden air.

The boy rowed easily, pulling as smoothly as if he had been at it all his life. But the island did not seem to come much closer. After a while he leaned on his oars to watch the shadow of the western hills touch and darken it. The boat swung slowly around and they drifted with the current. The little girl followed his gaze.

"Could we go *there?*" There was wonder in the question.

"I don't see why not," he said slowly, and then more firmly, "I don't see why not. Tomorrow. We'll go tomorrow. We might even make a camp. If I did it properly, no fires or anything, I don't think anybody would mind. We'll have a look tomorrow, anyway. And some day," he said softly, like a promise to himself, "some day I am going to sail down through the lock and down to the Mississippi and the sea."

It was while they drifted in toward the bank that a rising breeze riffled the pages of the old story from under the too-small stone and into the river, and it was gone. Gone, but not lost, for, not long after, Dave wrote down as much of it as he could remember. And if in later years it seemed to him that it had after all been no more than a dream, at least he never grew so old that he made the mistake of forgetting that dreams hold their share of truth, and that the deepest wisdom of dreams is that waking joys are deeper yet.